# FINDING THE NORTH WIND

## Book III of the Search and Rescue Dog Series

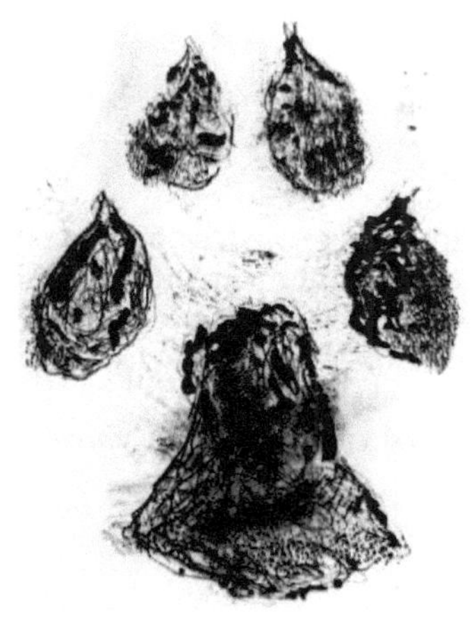

# SCOTT HAMMOND

Black Rose Writing | Texas

This is a work of fiction. Names, characters, businesses, places, events, and incidents are either the products of the author's imagination or used in a fictitious manner. Any resemblance to actual persons, living or dead, or actual events is purely coincidental.

ISBN: 978-1-68513-548-5
PUBLISHED BY BLACK ROSE WRITING
www.blackrosewriting.com

Printed in the United States of America
Suggested Retail Price (SRP) $17.95

*Finding the North Wind* is printed in Minion Pro

*As a planet-friendly publisher, Black Rose Writing does its best to eliminate unnecessary waste to reduce paper usage and energy costs, while never compromising the reading experience. As a result, the final word count vs. page count may not meet common expectations.

# FINDING THE
# NORTH WIND

# CHAPTER 1

"Kwayah."

The name tip-toed off her tongue into the autumn air then was stolen by the breeze.

The old woman, again. Softly. "Kwayah."

The child stood by the river with her grandmother and received her second naming. Fall leaves drifted in the ripples. In a quiet voice that penetrated the sound of rushing water, her grandmother placed the sacred name between them. Then she squeezed the girl's trembling hand.

"In your first naming, you are Que-am-arr. You were born on the day the seasons changed, so you are The North Wind. Now your second naming is what you are becoming. You are the runner."

The elders' words came to her eight-year-old granddaughter's ears, into the young one's heart, and were engraved on her soul.

"When the North Wind blows…" Her lips and bottomless brown eyes were all that moved on her sun-leathered face. "Kwayah-ci will run home." She added "ci" to the end of the word which was a story teller's way of claiming the name for her heart.

Her whispers still rolled like distant thunder fifteen years after the unforgettable conversation.

Prisoner 157 looked through the window and bars at the half-light scene unfolding before her then read again the postcard she received that day from the woman she called Grandma Wici. Her once eloquent cursive letters were now barely legible in their trembling arthritic flow of broken characters. It had no return address. No name. On the front was a picture of a generic Indian, not her tribe, in front of a street sign that said, "Welcome to Indian Country." On the back was the address of the Wyoming State Women's Prison Minimum Security Unit in Evanston, Wyoming. The text box simply said, "Child of the North Wind, come home."

The late day October sunlight half-heartedly poured into the room through the age-flawed glass that distorted the rays and formed a flowing zebra pattern mural on the far side wall. The rusted bars on the south-facing window discouraged uninvited visitors and reminded the minimum-security inmates that leaving would cost them another year or two of incarceration. Any inmate who had spent time pacing the room or piled on one of the old couches knew how to escape. They talked about it all the time. Few ever did it. Escaping the building would be relatively easy. But Evanston was a small town, and the gun-toting citizens had little sympathy for a woman dressed in an orange jumpsuit. The transcontinental railroad line passed through town, but that was the first place authorities would look for an escaped inmate. The second place would be the truck stops that serviced I-80. To the north were the plains of Wyoming. Open and obvious, with no cover from the wind. To the south and east were the High Uintahs, a west-to-east mountain range with most peaks above ten thousand feet.

But the real reason inmates did not escape was because they had no place to go. Most of the women, who called themselves "girls," came from Wyoming families and communities who had turned their backs on them. In some cases, they were forgotten. In other cases, the people on the outside didn't want to remember. An inmate's release and return might be unwanted by the children they had neglected, the husbands they had harmed, or the family they had exploited for drug money or booze.

But not for Prisoner 157. Her three-year-old daughter, aided by Grandma Wici, sent drawings every week. Her grandmother also often sent care packages with buffalo jerky and photographs since Prisoner

157 had no access to the internet. Sometimes tribal elders and her parish church members visited, even though it was a long, five-hour drive from the reservation. The support Prisoner 157 received from her community did not go unnoticed by her fellow inmates. Most were quietly envious. Some were openly hostile.

"You think you're so special just because you're an Indian!"

A week before, a white inmate from Rock Springs who was twice her size shouted in her face in an effort to bully her into a fight. "Yes," Kwayah thought. "I am special. My Grandma Wici and my daughter make me so." But she said nothing. Without facial expression, she stood her ground and looked directly into the eyes of the bully. Her stare froze her opponent long enough for the guard to run down the hall and into the recreation room.

She stood between the two women. "Who started this?" the guard, who was just out of community college, asked in her biggest voice. She was trying to sound authoritative but sounded more like an underage babysitter.

"I did," Prisoner 157 said in a quiet voice, surprising everyone. She didn't break eye contact with the aggressor.

"Why? What did you say?"

"I didn't say anything. She's mad at me because I'm an Indian."

Not knowing how to respond, the guard suddenly took an interest in the shine on her black leather boots. After a pause, she said, "You two finished?"

There was another pause as the stare between the two rivals unwound. Then they broke their gaze, and both walked slowly away from each other. A truce for now. Kwayah had dealt with bullies before. The big girl bully needed a target to show she was tough. Powerful. In charge. Being an Indian woman, Kwayah was different, so she was the target. It was just a matter of time before the volcano of violence would erupt. But Kwayah would never fight. She was small. Fast and elusive. Like the north wind. She would never allow herself to be caught in the grasp of the big, slow, angry woman.

And now, a week later, Prisoner 157 walked unacknowledged into the recreation room where tall windows framed the golden-brown northern Wyoming plains. The bully and her posse either didn't notice her or were too interested in the television program. With Prisoner 157's back to the crowd, she faced the poorly caulked old wood frames. When a gust of north wind rattled the glass, she felt the cold air leaking on her cheeks. In the brief moment, she could smell the grasses and sage and the sweet aroma of liberty.

"Kwayah," she whispered after the next gust as if she was responding to a question in the wind. "Please lead me home."

Below her, the once-green grass on the recreation field had already turned brown. The browning started with an inch of snow that fell a week earlier. It had melted by noon but signaled an early winter. Just a few days before, the hunting parties had come home from the hills with their deer. The guards talked a lot about hunting. It seemed like everyone who worked for a living in Evanston also hunted for meat. Venison. Elk. Wild turkeys. They hunted in Wyoming and over the border in Utah just ten miles away. They also fished until the ice that now rimmed the low-running streams froze over. Every year it was the same. The warm wind from the south would shift. Then the north wind began to blow, and the first snow would appear. Just a hint of real winter that would remind people it was time to stay home and cut wood for the fireplace.

Oblivious to the outside world, the inmates made the most of their last hour of television, watching a rerun of *Gilmore Girls*. As the episode ended, and the "girls" began to argue about Rory and Lorelai, the night shift guards started arriving in the parking lot below the Indian woman. Almost automatically, the "girls" sensed the change and lined up for the night shift inmate count. The night shift was as different from the day shift as day is from night.

The day shift in the minimum-security prison was presided over by Warden Daisey Mae Cromwell. Cromwell was a former US Marine sergeant who had distinguished herself in combat in Iraq. After military service, she took a job at the Wyoming State Penitentiary in Rawlings where she busted a prison drug smuggling ring and earned quick promotion. To reward her, and protect her from retaliation from the prisoners and guards in the drug ring, Cromwell was transferred into the small minimum-security facility in Evanston eighteen months ago as a warden. After moving across the state to Evanston, she changed everything. Prisoners were now supposed to be referred to by name not number. Mornings were spent doing chores, therapy, vocational training, and even university credit classes. For every hour spent doing something positive, you could have an hour of television, or earn the opportunity to attend church on Sunday, or even, in rare cases, the chance to go on a field trip.

Warden Cromwell insisted on being called "Daisey Mae." Her first project was to "encourage" the staff to adopt a different vision of prison life. Some did. Others were guided toward different careers or early retirement. Meanwhile, Daisey Mae hired guards, cooks, and therapists, and insisted they know all the "girls" by name. Daisey Mae would often stop inmates in the halls and engage them in conversation. Most inmates were suspicious at first but now felt comfortable crying on her shoulder when divorce papers were served or when incarcerated boyfriends announced they were moving on. Daisey Mae created a positive culture in a place where hope was scarce and honesty was rare. She had even become an advocate for some in parole hearings and helped inmates after they were released to get jobs and rebuild family relations. But as much light as she brought to the daily operation of the prison, Sergeant Dana Gare brought darkness during the night shift.

Sergeant Gare, as she insisted on being called, was more like a gang boss than a prison guard. She had avoided Daisey Mae's purge, protected by Human Resources, by staying systematically over-compliant with all prison policies and regulations. Over the years, as many other guards left for better jobs in better places, she had risen through the ranks, protected by a small group of guards she had personally hired. In a town where good-paying jobs were scarce, Gare found positions for drinking buddies, neighbors, and distant relatives. Now she protected her position by doing exactly what the warden and her staff wanted when they were watching, but when the "enlightened staff" left the building, she enacted her little cold war of abuse driven by her own life of disappointments. As soon as Daisey Mae and the day shift exited the building, the night shift began with a lineup in the recreation room. Sergeant Gare stood holding a clipboard in front of fifty-three inmates. They began by shouting out their numbers in order.

"Prisoner 005," the ritual began. She was serving a life sentence for murdering her abusive boyfriend. "Prisoner 009." She had driven the car in an armed robbery. "Prisoner 013." The bully had killed a young couple while driving under the influence of drugs. "Prisoner 157" was near the end. She was twenty-two months into a two-year sentence for assaulting her late husband's business associate. The business had been making and selling methamphetamine on the reservation. The associate was her late husband's chemical supplier who was pressing her to pay his debts in an illegal business she had nothing to do with. The assault had been self-defense. Just six weeks after her husband disappeared, the "associate" had come by to collect money. When she had forced him at gunpoint out of her house and away from her baby, he came back with a corrupt policeman who charged her with assault.

She could not afford an attorney, so the court appointed an attorney, who did little to help her defense. It was a rubber stamp justice system in the county court that saw it as just another drug-related crime in a community struggling to protect its people from the encroaching meth labs and drug dealers circling like hungry coyotes. Her lawyer talked her into signing a plea agreement and serving two years in prison. He said if she did not, she was sure to be convicted by her "peers" in a jury trial and serve ten years. "Every potential juror knows someone who has overdosed on meth," he argued. "They want to blame someone, and that someone is you."

One reason she took the deal was because her "peers" were not her peers. They were her husband's people. She was the outsider. He was dead. No one stood by to protect her or speak for her. The day before she reported to prison, she drove through the night with her sleeping child to Ohma, the safe home of the grandmother she admired. "We will cherish this little one until the North Wind comes home," she said, smiling a rare smile. "Now go and do what you must do." The tears would wait until she was alone in the car. Kwayah kissed her baby and her grandmother then drove five hours to Rawlins, Wyoming, where she sold her car for half its value to an opportunistic used car dealer, placed the money in an envelope, and sent it to her Ohma. Then she took an Uber to the prison, walked in the gate, and reported for her sentence.

The prison guard in charge of orienting new prisoners was a guard named Daisey Mae Cromwell. She had a vision of prison life that was not anything like what was really going on in the social sewer of the Rawlins women's prison. Kwayah was surprised when, just three months into her sentence, she was transferred to the minimum-security prison in Evanston on the other side of the state. And she was even more surprised to see Cromwell as the newly appointed warden.

Now, with two months left in her sentence and an endorsement from Cromwell to the parole board, Kwayah knew she would be disappointing her greatest, perhaps her only, advocate. As she stood watching the shift change a floor below, the warden walked out the front door of the tired old building, briefcase in hand. As she turned and unlocked her car, she hesitated, sensing she was being watched. She turned and looked up at Kwayah who had not moved from her window viewpoint. There was a nod and a smile, and she piled into her driver's seat and left the problems of the prison behind. Kwayah did not acknowledge her.

Kwayah shifted her gaze from the north-facing window and looked down on the rooftops of Evanston, Wyoming. She could see the train yard, the freeway, and the fast-food places. Parts of the town had not changed in eighty years. Except there was a black ribbon that split the town called I-80. The steady flow of traffic made Evanston a milestone for most but not a destination. More people passed through every day on the freeway or Amtrack than populated the town. They would leave their money behind in the rest stops at convenience stores, gas stations, and the fast-food restaurants that provided most of the nongovernment jobs since the oil drilling went away.

She caught the reflection of her long black hair in the imperfect glass of the old window. She had not aged, but she had lost weight. She was down to the same weight she had in high school when she was known. Before she had been forgotten. In the gloaming, as the clouds caught the setting sun and pushed the light down into the golden grasses, she looked past the town to the northern horizon. The scene was split by the moving lights along the northern highway leading to the plains of Wyoming. The plains of sorrow where her life had turned bad. The north wind coming off the flat lands of Canada, across the plains of Montana and Wyoming, would hit the Uintahs and push south. The wind at her back would take her home—to a better life, to her people, to say goodbye to her grandmother. Then whatever happened, she would be whole again. She would be able to face whatever this broken system was giving her. But first, she must run with the Kwayah.

Sally was Kwayah's cellmate. At ten p.m., they lined up in front of their doors for a second roll call. Gare would walk down the hall as if she was inspecting each of the inmates. As she passed, if she didn't pick on an inmate for some minor rules infraction or a violation of an imaginary dress code, she would say, "Okay," and that was the inmate's signal to step into her dorm room (what was called the "cells") until morning room call at seven a.m. For nine hours they would be in lockdown behind wooden doors, drafty windows, and rusty bars.

It was well rehearsed. As Gare passed and said, "Okay," Sally and Kwayah would step back, and Sally would go into the neighboring dorm room with another inmate who was her "friend." The guard who followed Gare down the hall winked. A few dollars or a pack of cigarettes, and a cover story of not getting along with Kwayah, bought Sally the opportunity for a sleepover two or three nights a week. Those were the nights Kwayah had been making her preparations. Making cuts in the already weathered calking around the windows so that they could be opened. Loosening up the rusty bars and weaving the rope from the old bed sheets.

As Sally initiated her deception, Kwayah stepped into her room and closed the door. The trailing guard locked it behind her. She sat on the bed, listening for the nightly lock-up ritual to end. After a few long minutes, she turned off her room light so she could see when the hall light was turned off. When it was, still she waited until the sounds outside told her the guards and the inmates were settled in for the night. She waited again until Gare stepped out the front door, placing a chair as a doorstop so she wouldn't need to use her key card to get back in. Then she lit a cigarette, inhaling the poison smoke deeply. She would do it in two-hour intervals until morning roll call.

When she was done smoking, she stepped back inside and closed the door. Kwayah quietly opened her window. Scanning for any unexpected onlookers, she pulled the old frame up and slid the center rusted bar out of place. This created just enough of a gap for her to leverage her petite frame through as she grasped the intact bars on each side. She had rehearsed these moves in her mind for months. She then stepped out onto the window ledge, reaching back inside to pull the homemade rope from behind the old radiator that was under the window. Then she carefully looped it around the other firm bars and dropped both ends to the ground. Still balancing on the ledge, with one hand clasping the firm bars, she closed the window from the outside then replaced the loose bar so that only a close inspection would reveal an escape. There was no going back now.

She grasped the rope, her grip holding both sides together, and made a sloppy rappel twelve feet to the ground. Landing in the soft soil, she pulled one side of the rope and let it drop to the ground. Then she used it to rough the soil so her footprints could not be easily seen. Then she stepped into the grass.

Holding the rope, she bolted towards the fence, pulling herself up and over in one motion. On the far side, she was finally in the shadows, and she relaxed just long enough to turn and see if she had triggered any alarms. Nothing. She had a six, maybe seven-hour head start.

She turned her back on the light of the prison and let her eyes adjust to the dark. As she did, a breeze from the north brought a chill to her spine. She hesitated, then stepped into the long grass and was gone.

# CHAPTER 2

Wyoming has two international airports, according to long-time residents. One in Denver and the other in Salt Lake City. The first time Caleb visited Nate and Marie, he flew into Denver then traveled to Lincoln, Wyoming, by bus and car. The second time, he avoided the six-hour drive across the state and caught a smaller regional flight to Rock Springs. That cut the drive time in half. This time it was cheaper to go through Salt Lake. Cheap was his parents' only criteria. His father was in graduate school. His mother worked on commission selling real estate in a slow market. And he was lucky to have any adventure that required money.

Today, his host, friend and mentor Deputy Nate Garner, would drive a couple hours to Evanston, Wyoming, then down I-80 for ninety minutes to the Salt Lake International Airport. Because he lived in Wyoming, a three-hour drive was not considered long. But Nate didn't like the city. And he especially didn't like the resort town of Park City, Utah, that he would pass through on the way to Salt Lake. "Too much like Jackson, Wyoming," he said, "where the self-important, privileged people build big houses that they visit annually, drive big cars, then criticize ranchers and farmers for ruining the environment." Nate planned to hold his nose as he passed through Park City. At the airport, he would pick up Caleb and turn around and head back to Wyoming immediately. Once they made it to the first real rural town of Coalville, Utah, they would stop at Ed's Spick and Span Diner for a breakfast to die for. It would be cooked by Jose, who bought the diner from Ed twenty years ago and kept the name because he couldn't afford new signage.

Caleb watched as the jet broke through clouds at 24,000 feet. He quickly oriented himself by picking out landmarks. They had passed over Lincoln in the clouds and now were descending along the I-80 corridor. Ed's Spick and Span Diner was about eighteen thousand feet below, somewhere along that black ribbon of asphalt, in a town next to a lake. Nate was guiding his Lincoln County Sheriff's vehicle down that same freeway, probably listening to the best of Johnny Cash on his early generation iPod. The two-hour flight from Iowa had been rough. Up and down as the plane dodged the thunderstorms on the Great Plains then hit a storm front stirred up by the peaks of the Wind River Mountain Range. As the plane dropped over the Wasatch range and into Salt Lake, it bounced through more turbulence. Then the flight smoothed out as it crossed the Wasatch and dropped into the Valley of the Great Salt Lake.

Caleb was one of the last passengers off the plane because he was an unattended minor and needed a flight attendant to watch his every move. "Like a prisoner transfer," the young boy thought. The flight attendant on the plane had been kind. Full of smiles as she brought him extra snacks and showed him how to use the in-flight feature on the video monitor that tracked the progress of the plane as if he was a pilot. But once this kind flight attendant said, "Goodbye," and signed him over to the ground service agent, he was just a piece of luggage with legs. The only thing the agent said was, "Follow me."

After a long walk following two steps behind his minder, they found the baggage claim monster, a polished steel merry-go-round spreading the luggage out for the waiting and weary passengers. The familiar faces from the plane snatched their belongings awkwardly and dragged them to groups of waiting friends and family. Caleb watched the scene and acknowledged his mother was right to have him carry on the plane his meager three fresh T-shirts, clean socks and underwear, toothbrush, and extra bootcut Levis in his school backpack. He had to leave his math textbook home to make room for the clothing in his carry-on. His homework would have to wait. Gosh, darn!

For five minutes, while the disinterested attendant texted on his cell phone, Caleb watched the luggage claim dance. Small people attempting to pluck massive suitcases from the moving machine. Emotional reunions. Fly fishermen guarding their gear like it was a treasure. A woman waiting and worrying she had been forgotten. It was the kind of real people scene that was better than any of the movies he had watched on the plane.

Then he heard the clickity clack of dog paws on a hard tile floor. As he looked up, Caleb heard a loud, angry voice near the exit door proclaim, "Hey!" Then he watched as people scattered, making way for a flash moving in his direction. As the sound of long dog paws tap-dancing on the slick floor grew louder, Caleb could see surprise and smiles on the faces of people as they leaned out of the way.

The attendant looked up and gave a little shriek, just in time to see a large, out-of-control golden retriever dashing through the parting crowd. "Holy…" He didn't finish his sentence. Like he was on ice, Boo could not fully stop on the slick floor. He slid into Caleb who knocked over the attendant and sent his cell phone sliding like a hockey puck into the crowd of waiting passengers. But before Caleb hit the ground, he was laughing as a tongue emerged from the big ball of fur and began licking his face. Meanwhile, the extremely annoyed attendant dropped to his hands and knees amongst the laughing crowd, looking for the phone with the unfinished text.

Lincoln County Wyoming Deputy Sheriff Nate Garner was right behind the dog, apologizing to anyone who was paying attention. He had evoked the special privileges that come with a marked police car and parked at the curb just outside the terminal door. He had rolled down the window to keep the cab cool for his search dog "Boo," but the dog caught the scent of his favorite friend among the hundreds of passengers. He couldn't control himself and bolted through the open back window and into the terminal before the deputy could give him a "stay" command.

After a few seconds of puppy play on the floor of the crowded airport, Caleb realized everyone was looking at him, so he stood up just in time to take Nate's outstretched hand.

"There's my buddy!" Nate said with a broad smile on his face. Like most cops and men from Wyoming, Nate was usually reserved and private with his affection. But this time he used the handshake to pull Caleb into a brotherly hug. "Glad you could come," he said.

Nate made it sound like Caleb was doing him a favor to come. Caleb saw it as another rescue. Caleb's mother had won a Caribbean cruise as a reward from her part-time real estate work. It was a perfect chance for his mom and dad to repair some of the damage that his father's graduate school experience had done to their marriage. The trip was perfectly. The trip was perfectly timed for Fall Break in Iowa, a weeklong period when the schools closed so that his classmates, most of whom were from farm families, could help with the harvest.

Caleb had overheard the request his parents made to his grandma, who never said, "No," but didn't always say, "Yes." She was willing to care for the kids, but she said, "Caleb is a handful. You know he ran away that time." His grandma evoked the time two years ago when Caleb had run away from his Aunt Marge and was lost in the Wyoming wilderness for three days. Boo had found him, and Nate had rescued him. The dog and his master had been his dear friends ever since. "I don't know if I could forgive myself if…" While his grandmother's worry was ill founded, that worry turned into another chance for Caleb to hang out with Nate and Marie and the wonderful dog named "Boo" that he called his best friend. He didn't know it was his grandmother who had ponied up airfare to send Caleb to stay in his summer hangout in Lincoln, Wyoming, with his Aunt Marge. In truth, he snubbed Aunt Marge and Cousin Billy and spent his days and some nights at the home of Nate and Marie. Now, two months after his summer ritual, he was getting a one-week fall bonus.

The attendant had collected himself and his phone and turned to Nate with a combination of anger and suspicion. "Are you Nathan

Garner of Lincoln, Wyoming?" he said, apparently thinking the sheriff's uniform was an elaborate early Halloween costume.

"I am." The deputy smiled and produced a very official Wyoming Police identification from his wallet with his badge. Then he called, "Boo," and pointed at his right leg. The dog immediately came to attention next to the deputy. The attendant produced a paper that needed signing, then folded it up, and without a thanks or any acknowledgement to Caleb, headed off to his next assignment.

"Let's get out of here before those Utah officers tow away my Wyoming Police vehicle," Nate said with a smile. Boo kept to his heel like he was on an invisible leash while Caleb walked on his other side, and the trio stepped out the door and into the cool, fall air. "We've got a long drive ahead of us," Nate said. "I'm thinking we visit Jose in Coalville on the way home. I'll bet you're hungry!"

"The mention of Jose reminded Caleb that the airline snacks had only taken the edge off his teenage hunger monster. "I sure am," he said with conviction then asked, "Where's Marie?"

"She had to work. But she also asked me to stop at Costco in Park City and load up on two of everything," Nate said in a joking tone. Caleb could see that his adult friend was really happy. So was he.

# CHAPTER 3

Between smoking breaks, Sergeant Gare spent most nights playing cards with the other guards, watching late night television, or listening to the UFO conspiracy theory radio. Once the prisoners were put to bed, they were supposed to only have contact with the guards if they got sick or in a fight. If an inmate pulled the alarm cord in their room, two guards would respond. Gare would follow as the enforcer. Often, she would ask to be left alone with the prisoner, dishing out more than words. Sometimes she would place inmates in the isolation cell then go back to cards or television. But some nights, Gare would watch as her loyal guards would torment the tormented. Gare had become an expert at using Cromwell's progressive rules as a means of torture. When she had come on board, Cromwell had eliminated the cleaning staff and placed the inmates in charge of keeping the ward clean. She also made a rule that an inmate could not leave her room until her bed was made. Gare leveraged these rules to systematically abuse the inmates, especially those who were different or vulnerable.

Once a week at midnight, when most prisoners were asleep, the night guards would have "mail call" and distribute items that family members had paid them to smuggle into the prison. The regular mail came every day, and the prison guards picked through the packages for contraband, sometimes taking items of value for personal gain or to use as psychological levers with the prisoners. The weekly letters and pictures from Kwayah's daughter were sometimes intercepted, until her grandmother started putting a twenty-dollar bill in the letter. When the envelope was opened, the money was pocketed, and the letter and drawings were passed on.

At first, guards justified the extra money because of the low wages. But then they became used to the extra two or three hundred in cash they each collected every week. They used the money to buy trucks or take trips they could not otherwise afford, and the "handling fees," they called it, became an entitlement. If prisoners didn't use the system, they were abused.

Kwayah's abuse began one night after she received a birthday care package from her grandmother without the "postage." She received the envelope under the door after lights out. With a small flashlight, she looked at her daughter's pictures and read the letter. Then Kwayah stashed the letters in her hiding place.

Just when she had returned to her bed, Gare pounded on her door and yelled in an accusatory tone, "There's a mess in the shower room. We need you to clean it up, now!" Out of habit, Kwayah made her bed. Then the door was unlocked, and she was escorted to the shower room only to find an unspeakable mess that took her an hour to clean up. While she was in the shower room, two guards were tossing her room and scattering her bed clothes across the floor. They said they were looking for her letter stash. When Kwayah was finished with the shower chores, they complained that her bed was not made. Sure enough, the bed covers were scattered around the room, as were the pictures drawn by her daughter. Afraid to complain, Kwayah made her bed and collected the items on the floor. Before she was finished, Gare was at the door again. "The shower room is still messy." Kwayah returned to the shower room only to find it messed up again. This cycle continued all night. Make your bed. Clean the shower room. The guards smirked. Gare scowled. Kwayah complied. The message was simple. We have the power. You do not.

Luckily, tormenting inmates was not on the agenda on the October night that Kwayah blew away. At the seven a.m. roll call, inmates were expected to have their beds made when their door was unlocked. Then they would stand outside their door as Gare would inspect their rooms. If she was in a black mood, she would give into her temptation to torment, step into a room, pull a few things on the floor, or mess up the bed.

On this October morning, the doors were opened, and Sally stepped into the hall, sliding next to the door where she expected to see Kwayah. It didn't take long for the guard to notice a missing inmate. "Who's missing?" she called.

"It's that damn Indian," Gare erupted. "Wake her up." She assumed Prisoner 157 had overslept. Sally stepped into the room where she was supposed to have slept and saw two beds made perfectly and no Kwayah. Gare stepped in behind her, and both women stood, jaws dropping to the floor, looking at two beds that had not been slept in.

Even though it was clear Kwayah was not in the room, the sergeant looked behind the radiator, the stainless-steel toilet, and under the beds. She pulled the mattresses off the bedframes, as if Kwayah might be hiding in the cot or bedding. She looked behind the door, all the time yelling at Sally and cursing the missing Indian woman. Sally said nothing because if she did, she would have to admit she had slept in a different room.

Gare took her tantrum into the hall and began yelling at the inmates and then the guards. Her anger was driven by fear of humiliation. She didn't want to face the popular and progressive Warden Cromwell and tell her one of the inmates was missing. It was 7:15 a.m., and Cromwell would be there at eight a.m. Gare ordered a search of every room. First, the guards went from dorm room to dorm room. Once each room was cleared, the occupants were questioned then locked back in their rooms. This took a full thirty minutes.

Finally, the night guards gathered at the end of the hall. With all the inmates once again confined in their night spaces, they began their search of the rec room, the shower room, the roof, the offices, everything. It was a panic driven search. Gare would rather drink turpentine than expose her incompetence to Cromwell.

When the 8:00 a.m. hour came and Cromwell arrived at work on time, she came face-to face with the frantic searchers. Gare made her confession while everyone on the night shift and the day shift watched. Cromwell listened calmy then said, "Show me her room." Gare unlocked the room Kwayah shared with Sally, and Cromwell signaled Gare to stay outside. The warden stepped into the room where Sally was sitting on the edge of her bed because she didn't want to have to make it again.

"You didn't sleep in here last night, did you?" the warden said in a friendly voice.

"No," Sally felt safe to admit.

"When did you last see her?"

"At night roll call last night."

"Thank you, Sally," the Warden said in a calm voice.

Cromwell stepped over to the window and looked out across the yard, the ranches, and the flat lands to the Uintah Mountains with their first dusting of snow. In this old building, all the old wooden windows had seventy years of paint covering a bad caulking job. Inmates complained on hot summer days when the few ceiling fans just pushed the super-heated air around, but no cool air could enter. She looked closely at the window. There was a razor cut line around the frame. With the flick of a wrist, she pulled up the window. The cold north wind hit her in the face and stirred loose objects in the room. Then she reached for the bars. The first one she tested in the middle was loose, and with another small effort, she pulled it out and set it on the floor of the dorm room.

The warden poked her head out the window and looked down. At the base of the wall, the soil was disturbed. Her ex-Marine eyes then turned to the grass. The angle of the morning sun was just right to see footprints in the still moist grass left from the morning dew. The footprints lead to the fence, to the fields, to freedom.

"Oh, Kwayah," she said under her breath. "What have you done?"

# CHAPTER 4

Caleb could barely contain his hunger as he followed Nate through the giant warehouse store. What kept the hunger monster at bay were the samples. Small portions, but free food on almost every aisle. To make the Costco run, Nate and Marie saved grocery money for months. Then they would make the trip to Park City and buy the bulk size packages that lasted longer and allowed them to stay stocked up for the winter. Nate was kind of glad Marie was not with him because there would be no good-deal impulse buys that stretched an already tight budget.

From Costco in Park City, it was just thirty-five minutes to Coalville and Ed's Spick and Span Diner, but Caleb's stomach growled all the way, and Nate teased him about it.

"Hey, could you keep the stomach of yours quiet? I can't hear the radio." Caleb laughed.

"Nate! Welcome." The deputy was warmly greeted by the waitress Jeanie. Then she looked at Caleb and said in a sarcastic tone, "Another prisoner transfer?" Nate laughed and told Caleb he stopped at the diner every time he transferred a prisoner to the FBI field office in Salt Lake.

As if she could read the hunger in Caleb's eyes, Jeanie asked if they wanted "the usual," and Caleb and Nate nodded, though Caleb had no idea what the usual might be. It was close to midday, and the worn-out restaurant with the worn-out booths with taped-over red cracking and benches was already filling up with working men wanting a big lunch.

But breakfast was always on, and Jeanie was quick to produce a super-sized plate with two eggs, two long strips of thick-sliced bacon and a sausage patty, hash browns, a biscuit, and coffee for Nate. Caleb settled for a coke. After a minute, Jeanie produced a plate stacked high with pancakes and a sticky pitcher of maple syrup. "Jose wanted me to bring you these and thank you for your service in law enforcement," she said, knowing that Caleb would likely consume them all. Nate nodded thanks and pushed the pancakes towards Caleb who reached for the syrup with one hand and his fork with another.

When the breakfast platters were finished and Caleb had reduced the stack of pancakes by half, Nate's cell phone rang. The screen said Rondo Mathews. "That's strange. It's my buddy who's the sheriff in Uintah County in Evanston. Maybe he wants to know where the fish are biting in Lincoln County."

"Hi, Rondo," he answered.

"Hey, Nate." Pause. There was no small talk, signaling this was not a social call. "You got your dog with you?" he asked.

"Sure. What's up?"

"Well, we have a unique situation going on, and I need your dog."

Nate chuckled. "So, you only love me for my dog."

"That's right," Rondo said in an upbeat voice. "I've got several officers out sick, and the rest are busy keeping the department from going under. We do have our certified police dog with its handler, but all he's good for is finding drugs and biting people."

"Okay," said Nate.

"Anyway. We have a minimum-security women's prison on the campus of the old state hospital just south of town."

Nate could see what was coming. An escaped prisoner.

Rondo continued, "We never have any trouble because, well, it's minimum security and these gals, women, I should say, most of them just have a short time before they're released. The rest don't have homes or families or boyfriends to go home to. So, escapes are rare, and the security is pretty light. I mean it's almost like a halfway house."

"Someone ran?" Nate pushed the conversation along as Caleb pushed more pancakes into his mouth.

"Yeah," said Rondo. "I've been on this police force for twenty years, and I don't remember once having a missing prisoner. We had a couple runners from the old days when the mental hospital was in operation. But not since it was converted to a prison. Women prisoners just don't escape."

"How can we help?" Nate said.

"I know Boo is a great tracking dog, Nate. And that's what I need. He found that kid a few years ago after three days, right?"

"Yup." Nate smiled and looked at Caleb who was busy shoveling pancakes into his mouth.

"Well, the runner in this case is not dangerous, and the warden tells me she doesn't want our rather aggressive police dog after her. Could you help?"

"How long has she been gone?"

"Near as we can tell, since about two a.m. So, about ten hours."

"Do you have a point-last-seen and scent articles?" Nate asked, his mind kicking into gear.

"Yup."

"Anyone to help me?" Nate asked.

"That's the tricky one," the police chief said. "I've got a half dozen of the night guards from the prison who were already organizing a search when I was called. They had everything ready except the hood and burning torches," he said in a sarcastic tone. "Daisey Mae says she does not want her people involved in a search."

"Daisey Mae?" Nate interrupted.

"Yes," said Rondo. "Daisey Mae Cromwell is the warden. She says the guards are not trained for pursuit, but I also think she's afraid of what will happen if they catch her. Some of them had their hunting rifles racked up in their trucks."

"Who are we tracking?" Nate asked.

"A young woman, an Indian woman from the reservation. Married to a meth head and cooker who was probably murdered, but no charges were brought. She was accused of assaulting the drug supplier, and the judge went easy and gave her two years. She just has a few months left on her sentence. By all accounts, she has been a model prisoner. Did some training. Earned an Emergency Medical Technician certificate even though they wouldn't let her register because she was in jail."

"Any idea where she's headed?"

"Probably back to the reservation. Whenever we get Indians through town, they're usually headed back to the res. They follow the rail line east for a few hundred miles to Rock Springs or Rawlins then head north. They try to hop on one of the moving trains, and the Union Pacific guards rarely catch them."

Nate looked over at Caleb who was listening to every word. "I've got our nephew with us." Nate often embellished their relationship because most people required a much longer explanation if you said you had a young helper with you. "He's helped us out before. He's really good with the dog…"

Rondo cut Nate off. "Is he the one who rescued that autistic boy ahead of the Feds last summer?"

"Sure is." Nate smiled at Caleb who had now finished the stack of pancakes.

"And the boy Boo found after three days."

"Yes."

"You trust him?"

"Sure do," said Nate.

"All right. I think this will go pretty quickly, and it will be good to have another set of eyes. But keep him safe, Nate. I don't want an incident. I hope this will be over by tonight."

"You know my dog is not aggressive," Nate reminded Rondo. "He can track her, but he won't bring her down like a police canine. He's a search and rescue dog. So, I will need to arrest her. It might be good to have a female officer there."

"I know, I know." Rondo said. "I don't have any women deputies. But the warden is an ex-Marine, and she says she can go with you.

"Daisey Mae is an ex-Marine?"

"She's someone I admire," said Rondo. "I like what she's doing with these women. She tells me to find her and go easy, and that means a SAR dog."

"I'll have to clear it with my sheriff," Nate said.

"I already have," Rondo said.

"Then I'll see you in about an hour." Nate terminated the call.

After hanging up, Nate immediately explained the big change of plans to Caleb, thinking the boy might be disappointed. But nothing could be further from the truth. Caleb was excited because he would be going on another adventure with Boo and Nate, this time tracking an escaped prisoner. He had helped Nate with searches for lost people before. He loved it when Nate turned on the flashing lights and pulled people over when they were speeding or had run a red light. Once, he had even seen Nate arrest someone at a traffic stop who appeared to be drunk. Another sheriff's deputy had arrived as back-up and took the man to jail. Caleb had never been on a fugitive search, and it seemed like it would be more fun than any of preplanned fun Nate and Marie had put together for this visit. Still, Caleb reacted like a lot of teenage boys would, with muted enthusiasm. After all, he had to stay cool.

"I guess so," he said.

"Cool," Nate said then turned his attention to his cell phone where the notes and report of the incident were pouring into his text box. After a few clicks, he said to Caleb, "Do you want to see who we're looking for?" The photo was neutral, like most police photos, but Caleb could see that she was quite pretty. She was small. Petite. Soft brown eyes that showed quiet confidence. Long black hair and soft brown skin. A native American.

"Not what I thought," Caleb said for both of them. He replaced the picture in his head—heavy, scared face, mean looking, tattooed, a shaved head. He was all wrong. She looked like someone's older sister.

As they exited the Spick and Span, Jose caught Nate in the small unpaved parking lot and handed him a bag of donuts and a bit of scrap meat for Boo. "No, no," said Nate. "The pancakes were enough." He feigned resistance but then took the bag when it was handed to him.

"Keep safe, my friend." Jose was a full head shorter than Nate. There was an awkward hug, and he also shook Nate's hand then turned to Caleb and addressed him like they were old friends.

"Take care of this guy, okay?"

"I will," said Caleb.

At the truck, Nate separated the meat scraps and put them in a plastic bag. "We'll use these to reward Boo when he finds the prisoner."

Caleb's eyes said he wanted more information.

"After two years in prison, this woman is probably out of shape. She left for no reason and is likely already regretting it. We need to keep our eyes open because she might already be trying to get back. I think Boo will find her pretty quickly, and we might even be home for a late dinner in Lincoln," he said with a smile. He texted Marie and told her what he had just told Caleb then started his truck and headed up I-80 through Echo Canyon to Evanston, Wyoming.

# CHAPTER 5

A brown, brick hospital building has been presiding on the hill over Evanston since 1899. Originally it was called an *asylum* for lunatics. Then a *hospital* for the insane. Later it was called a *facility* for the mentally ill. With each name change, a new set of ideas about how mental illness should be treated emerged. The early hospital had ice baths, where prisoners were strapped into a bathtub then covered up to their necks in ice water. Later, lobotomies were the fad, where a doctor would force a sharp object resembling an ice pick into the brains of patients. Then shock treatment was introduced, where electrodes were placed on the head and high voltage electricity disrupted brain cells, forcing the brain to reboot, hopefully in a better state. While shock therapy was still used in rare cases in modern times, most past treatments of the mentally ill had been abandoned because they were seen as ineffective at best, and barbaric at worse. The well-intentioned staff members, who really had very little to offer patients, went from hero to villain with each rewriting of history.

But in the 1960s, the development of psychotropic drugs meant much of the population of the Wyoming State Hospital could rejoin society. When the hospital population declined from 600 plus residents to below 100, the citizens of Evanston began to complain. They had come to rely on the jobs provided by the State Hospital. Politically savvy, cost-conscious law makers decided to use now vacant parts of the complex for a population that was growing—women who were serving prison terms. The cost of turning the old brown building into a fully secure prison was prohibitive, but making it into a dormitory-style minimum-security prison seemed like a political win-win. So "Old Brown," as it was called, was given new life as a minimum-security prison, overlooking the town, the train yard, the freeway, and the high plains. Some of the attendants from the mental hospital retrained and became prison guards because good jobs, with pensions, were hard to come by.

As Nate, Caleb, and Boo arrived onto the campus of the women's prison, they were surprised to find the electronic gate opened. Then they passed a guard shack that had been empty since the budget cuts a few years back. "If no one is escaping, why do we need a guard?" the previous warden had reasoned.

Nate drove a few hundred yards down a narrow drive to the parking lot in front of "Old Brown," only to find the lot was more than full of marked police cars and both shifts of prison guards. Nate parked his Lincoln County Sheriff's truck on the unkept grass next to other pickup trucks sprawled without order on the unkept lawn. He stepped out of the truck and told Caleb in his no-nonsense police voice, "Wait here. I'll go in and meet the warden and get our assignment. Then we'll get that dog going and make quick work of this." Then he smiled and said, "Marie is baking a pie for desert tonight, and I want to be there."

As he approached the main entrance, Nate could see police tape near the base of the east corner of the building below an open window one story up. That would likely be the starting point for his track, but he was disappointed with the care of the crime scene. He could see the area had been trampled, so there would be many scents for Boo to sort out before he could find the right track.

Boo whimpered and thrashed a bit with frustration. It was clear he had read the mood of the two humans and knew he was about ready to go to work. An impatient dog when things needed to be done, Boo let out an anxious bark.

As Nate walked up the uneven concrete path towards the entrance to the prison, a small group of women guards coming off duty exited the building. Their khaki shirts were wrinkled, and their faces showed their fatigue, but they were in a fully animated conversation. As he walked past, Nate said, "Hello." Nothing. Either they didn't notice Nate, or they didn't want him to be noticed. But they were speaking loud enough that it was clear they wanted someone to hear. They were clearly feeling bold. Nate wondered if they would be so bold if they weren't in a group.

"She thinks she's in control of this place, but she's not."

"Yeah. Her favorite little Indian princess has flown the coup, and she wants to blame us."

"Prisoner 157," spoken like the name was poison, "chose our watch to bolt so we ought to have the first chance at finding her," said the only one in full uniform. She was a short, very stout woman with an "in your face" demeanor, even with her colleagues. "I'd go find her myself, but Daisey Mae," her voice was dripping in sarcasm when she said the name, "says I need to work tonight. In four hours!

Another guard piped in, "Our princess has probably hoped a train and is halfway to Cheyenne by now. They'll pick her up on the Indian res, or she'll overdose when she gets her first high," another said with contempt.

"I understand they have some hot shot tracker coming in from another county because Daisey Mae doesn't want a real police dog going after her," a third said.

They continued to vent even as they separated into their various vehicles in the parking lot. Nate figured that was the night shift who had been talking to investigators all morning and into the early afternoon. Based on their attitude, he figured they would be taking out their frustrations on the prisoners who didn't escape on their upcoming night shift. Meanwhile, the young woman who did escape was getting further away all the time, though Nate assumed she was probably hiding in a shed or abandoned building. She likely would not be running, he thought. Most prisoners were overweight and out of shape. And this search might be over before dark.

As he stepped into the building, he was immediately greeted by a tall, fit woman who reached for his hand with confidence and said, "Hi, I'm Daisey Mae." Her grip was strong, and her smile was sincere, and Nate instantly liked her. "Thanks for coming," she said and motioned him to a couch in the waiting room.

"How did you like our welcoming committee?" she said with a sparkle in her voice.

Nate smiled. "They're not happy campers."

"Yes," said the warden. "I'm making them all work tonight so they don't go out looking for our escapee. But I expect that in the next few minutes, some of them will start calling in sick."

Nate smiled again.

"Then they'll get their boyfriends' deer rifles and start driving around the county and looking in their neighbor's barns."

"Not good," Nate said.

"So, let's get you started and try to wrap this up as soon as possible," the warden said.

"Okay," said Nate. "But first, can you give me a little background?"

Daisey Mae had a well-rehearsed speech about the missing woman that she clearly had already given a dozen times that day. "Her legal name on court documents is Mandy Thunder Cloud. But no one even knows that. She goes by Kwayah. As far as we know, she has no local relatives or connections. She's twenty-four years old, five foot four inches, and has long black hair. I'm not sure of her current weight, but it's around 120 pounds."

Surprised, Nate said, "So, she's in pretty good shape?"

"Yes," said Daisey Mae. "She darn near wore out the treadmill we have in the exercise room. Every time someone was not on it, she would jump on. Some days she would run for three or four hours."

"Really?" Nate abandoned his assumption that she was out of shape.

"Yes. And she wasn't just jogging either. She's a runner."

Nate could see that Daisey Mae took fitness seriously, and he detected a hint of envy in her voice as she described the endurance and speed of the Indian woman.

"Where do you think she would head?" Nate asked, knowing Daisey Mae had probably spent a lot of time thinking about that.

"She has a kid and a grandmother she was close to. She was arrested on the Shoshone reservation just two years ago after her husband was murdered. I'm going to guess she's headed that direction. But it's four hundred miles or so. Either she had help and is in a car, or she's trying to hop the eastbound train and ride some of that distance, or she's going to try to do it by herself."

Nate jumped in, "I doubt she would attempt that distance on her own considering winter is just a few days away. We've already had some snow in the high country."

"I think you're right. So, we ought to start the dog here and see what happens. If we get a track to the road, then she had help and is in a car. If we get a track to the rail line, then she's on the rail. And I guess it's possible she's enjoying her freedom in an abandoned shed or something." Daisey Mae laughed just a little as she finished.

"Do you have any experience..." Nate regretted his question immediately and was cut off.

"Semper Fi." Daisey Mae pulled up her shirt sleeve and revealed a US Marine Corps tattoo. "I taught escape and evasion techniques in the California Desert for two years before I came home to Wyoming and started working in corrections. I haven't been on the pursuit end before, but I have been the runner.

"My parents named me Daisey Mae, hoping for a girly girl. They bought me dolls, but I wanted a toy gun because I played army with the boys. By the time I was a teenager, they gave up and accepted that I wanted to serve. I did twenty years with the Marines."

Nate was impressed as she turned the conversation to the task at hand.

"So, what do you need?"

"I need to start with a scent article."

"I've got one," Daisey Mae said, holding up a bag with a sock in it. "But it was collected by one of those night shift yahoos. Let's get you another one that your dog can rely on."

"Sounds good," said Nate. "Also, I have a young man with me who has helped me before…"

"Caleb?" said the warden.

"Yes," Nate said, surprised she knew his name.

"I remember his story in the media from a couple summers ago. Sounds like a great kid."

"He is, but I don't have time to take him back to Lincoln…," Nate began his explanation, but Daisey Mae cut him off.

"I think it will be great to have another set of eyes. Besides, Kwayah is not dangerous." She paused. "I have no idea why she's running."

# CHAPTER 6

Caleb had seen the green Wyoming. But this was brown Wyoming. The once green aspen had turned, with leaves painted bright yellow or red. The grass was golden brown and seemed to flow in waves like the ocean with the slightest breeze. The air was crisp, and even at midafternoon, he needed a jacket to take off winter's edge.

From his confinement in the pickup truck in the parking lot, Caleb could see Nate's head poke out from the east corner window. Boo saw him too, and he began to shake with anticipation. Nate looked around then looked southeast towards the Uintah Mountains. Nate pulled his head in, and within a few minutes, he was walking towards the truck with a large plastic bag in his hand with what looked like a sheet in it. Caleb knew enough to know it would be the scent article off the bed where the native woman slept. Boo would place his nose on it and remember the scent just like humans might remember a photograph. But unlike a photograph, the dead skin cells that gave this sheet its unique smell were also scattered along a trail where the fugitive had walked. It would not take long for Boo to find that track, and then he would obsessively follow the scent to the source.

Caleb had seen Boo track many times. In training, Caleb was often the runner. But last summer, at the urgent request of the Lincoln County Sheriff, Caleb used Boo to track an autistic boy named Asher to a wilderness lake. Caleb was excited to see Boo on this track. It was like there was a switch on this lazy, friendly dog. When you put him on a search command, he got an energy boost. Out of excitement, he often overran the track he was following. But he would self-correct and find the right track and follow it obsessively to the person they were searching for. Caleb wondered how this was going to go.

Nate emerged from the entrance to the prison, and a few steps behind him was a tall woman with a small backpack, gloves, a winter jacket, and hiking boots. She was talking with Nate as if they were old friends. Nate handed her the keys to his truck then opened the back door of the cab.

"Caleb, this is Warden Daisey Mae Cromwell. She's going to drive the truck while I track Boo. Are you okay to work with her?"

"Sure," Caleb said as the warden opened the driver's door and got in.

"Hi, Caleb," the woman said, smiling. "I guess I know more about you than you do about me."

"Oh?"

"I know you from that super survival story a few years ago, when you were in the wilderness for three days. I follow those kinds of things because I used to teach survival and evasion for the Marine Corps. You did everything right."

"I probably shouldn't have run away," Caleb noted, and Daisey Mae laughed.

"You okay riding with me while Nate works the dog?"

"Sure," said Caleb.

They watched as Nate put Boo on a long tracking lead. The two then walked over to the place where the fugitive had landed on the ground under the far east window. Boo looked like a loaded spring ready to release. As Nate asked the dog to sit, Boo quivered. Then he opened the plastic bag and exposed the scent article. As soon as Boo put his nose on the article, Nate gave the "track" command. The spring released, and

Boo sprang into action, nose down, crisscrossing the lawn in a weaving pattern, then locking into a path that headed in a southeast direction.

"I think he's already got her track," said Daisey Mae. "What an amazing dog."

*He is an amazing dog,* Caleb thought. He was too shy to engage with the warden just yet, but that was about to change.

# CHAPTER 7

Boo led Nate across the cut grass and right to the spot where the runner had stopped, planted her feet, and climbed the chain link fence. Nate could see the disturbed soil where she had launched from one side and landed on the other. At that point, Boo pawed at the fence, hoping to find a break. He was anxious to get back to tracking, but after a few slams with his paw and a nudge with his nose, he gave in and followed Nate to the front gate then around the perimeter of the fence back to the track.

As the deputy and the dog passed the pickup truck in the parking lot, Nate nodded at Caleb and Daisey Mae to get started. The plan was for the warden to drive while Caleb kept watch on Boo through a set of binoculars.

When Boo arrived back at the place where the fleeing woman had gone over the fence, he put his nose to the ground and began following her trail into the thick, golden grass and sagebrush. The scent trail made up of the dead skin cells the escapee left behind was about sixteen hours old. It would be an easy job for Boo. Tracking was his best skill, though Nate most often used him off lead in an area search. When Boo was looking for a missing person, he most often zigzagged through the search zone until he found a track then followed the scent to the person. But when it was a specific tracking situation, Nate would usually place Boo on a fifty-foot lead attached to his vest. Nate loved to work the dog where he could see him making directional decisions on an invisible scent line that led to the source.

With this situation, he began this track with the lead attached because the grass was tall enough he was afraid he would lose site of the energized dog. There had been times when Nate had attached a GPS collar to Boo, but the heavy collar and the antenna would inhibit the dog in tight places. So, Nate used a low-tech solution. He put a bear bell on the dog so he could hear him as he moved out of sight. Still, it was not uncommon for the bell to go missing or for Nate to find it in a tight spot snagged on a tree trunk.

But tracking with the lead was also difficult because of the sage and tall grass that kept snagging the leash and jerking the dog. After a while, Boo was annoyed with the pulls on his collar, and Nate was moving too slowly. So, Nate stopped, called Boo back, and unclipped the small carabiner that held the line to the collar. Boo immediately disappeared into the bushes, but he was easy to follow because he left a clear path on the ground, and Nate could hear the collar bell in the distance. He also could see the occasional footprint of the woman they were pursuing.

After following the track for about a half mile through dense brush, they broke through the brush and onto a double track trail. Daisey Mae and Caleb were already there in the pickup truck as they had anticipated the direction of travel. Boo was a couple hundred yards ahead, and as Nate broke out of the thicket, the dog paused, returned to his master, and touched his cold nose to Nate's palm. It was not something he was trained to do, but he often checked his partner and handler this way. Then he set the track direction again as if to say, "You all right, now hurry up!"

As Nate followed the dirt road towards the east, he wondered what the subject would do when she got to the river. Would she assume she was being tracked by a dog, jump into the current, and make the age-old mistake that flowing water is a barrier for tracking dogs? Or would she cross directly and continue east towards the railroad tracks? She did neither.

Without any effort to hide her tracks, the woman followed the fisherman's trail along the west side of the river. As Nate followed the muddy path along the bank, he began to feel like he was missing something. Why was the subject moving parallel to the railroad tracks but not going on the tracks? Why did she have such a deliberate direction? And finally, he observed her steps were equally spaced with a long stride. Why was she running? Given the length of the stride, Nate calculated that at the rate she was running, unless she stopped for a break, she was going twice as fast as they were tracking.

Nate pulled his hand-held radio off his belt and called Daisey Mae on the tactical frequency that was dedicated to their search. They were the only ones on the frequency, so the conversation was casual.

"Warden?" Nate began. "She's moving awfully fast, and she seems headed up valley."

There was a pause while the warden found her radio and responded. "What are you thinking?"

"I don't know this area well, but it seems to me she's using the thick trees and brush along the river for cover. She might be paralleling the river, or she might be headed to one of the ranches two or three miles up the river. Either way, she has a long stride and knows exactly where she's going. This is no ordinary…" Nate interrupted himself. "Boo has found something. He just did an alert, and he's taking me to… It's her shoe. She lost her shoe," Nate said with excitement. "That will slow her down," he added under his breath.

Daisey Mae gave Nate a half minute to start moving again then asked, "What does the track look like now?"

"Boo just found the other shoe. These cheap prison sneakers just couldn't hold up to her foot pounding. She wore them out in about two miles."

There was another pause.

"Damn!" The winded voice of Nate came back on the radio. Nate almost never uttered profanity. When he did, especially when he was around his wife Marie, she would stare darts at him until he apologized.

"She hasn't stopped running. Losing the shoes hasn't slowed her at all."

"That doesn't surprise me," said Daisey Mae. "She often ran barefoot on the treadmill in the exercise room even though we asked her to wear shoes. But she ran so much that we couldn't afford to keep her in shoes."

Nate continued to follow the runner along the river for a few hundred yards. Then he paused again.

"Warden, according to my map, there's a road that crosses the river about three miles ahead. I suggest you and Caleb drive to where the road hits the river and see if you can pick up a track along the road. My guess is there aren't too many barefoot joggers in this part of town."

"You got it," said Daisey Mae.

·  ·  ·

"So, Caleb, did you hear that? Can you direct me where we need to go?"

"Yes," Caleb said, smiling. He was warming up to Daisey Mae. In the short time they'd been together, she'd already asked his opinion two or three times, and she had asked him to check out things using the binoculars. Daisey Mae handed Caleb her cell phone with the SAR TOPO navigation system turned on and the track log engaged. He could see where they had been, but he could also see Nate's track log from his cell phone that was heading southeast. The warden pointed to the intersecting county road and said, "Navigate me to that intersection point. Let's see if we can jump ahead on this search."

After a difficult turn around and two separate gates with cattle guards, they pulled onto the highway and traveled a short distance before turning left onto a well-traveled gravel road. It cut across the valley going west to east and was the access road to three ranches, sporting cattle guards and well-kept fences on both sides.

After traveling a few hundred feet, Daisey Mae smiled and asked Caleb, "Can you do something very important for me? I want you to walk along the left side of the road and carefully watch for the footprints. Also, watch where she might have come over the fence and up to the road. I'll follow right behind driving very slowly."

At first, Caleb was dubious. He wondered if he would see the barefoot footprints that were now sixteen or seventeen hours old on the hard packed dirt and gravel. He walked slowly, as instructed, turning his head to the north, and following the fence line with his eyes. At one point, he stopped and looked far to the north where they had come from. Over a mile away, across the barbed wire fences of these ranch properties in the flat river bottoms, he could see a blond golden retriever weaving back and forth across the grass. Behind the dog, just emerging from a brush thicket on the river, was his friend Nate. Caleb instinctively extended his arm towards the trackers and, using it as a guide, followed the path of least resistance to the road he was standing on. The intersection he imagined was just 100 feet in front of him. He looked along the fence, and in a space between two poles, just a hundred feet away, he saw a piece of gray cloth twisted onto the barbwire. He stepped down from the road to the fence and approached the cloth. Like a little flag, it clearly marked a recent fence crossing that had caught clothing. In the muddy field, he could see long-stride human footprints coming towards him then over the fence, up the bank, and turning to the east along the road.

He looked at Daisey Mae who was idling the pickup with her head out the side window. She had seen it too, and she was smiling ear to ear. "Nice job!" she said with authority, giving all the credit to the young boy.

Daisey Mae picked up the radio and called Nate. "We have an intercept on County Road 152 about one mile to your south. We're going to man track until you catch up."

"Ten-four," Nate said. Caleb could tell he was trying to sound like he wasn't huffing and puffing to keep up with his dog.

Daisey Mae examined what was in front of them. "Either she has crossed the river up there, or she has gone into one of the ranches on this side of the river," Daisey Mae said. "She's got to be tired and wanting sleep and food. We'll check all the buildings if we have to."

"Boo can make quick work of that," Caleb reminded the warden.

She nodded and said, "Okay, let's see what the tracks tell us."

Daisey Mae kept her head outside the driver's side window and followed the track in the gravel to the driveway of the first ranch on the left. But now that he knew what to look for, Caleb could see it too, even though he was on the passenger's side of the cab. The warden observed aloud that unless she doubled back, Mandy clearly didn't stop there. The tracks continued and didn't change direction when they came to the second driveway on the right. Now the tracks were headed directly to the bridge that crossed the river. Daisey Mae scratched her head. "I wonder why she's not trying in the least to hide her direction."

The bridge was paved, and no tracks led across the bridge. But Daisey Mae and Caleb both quickly spotted tracks on the other side of the river heading directly for a lone house. Daisey Mae picked up the radio. "She crossed the river at the bridge and appears headed towards the only ranch house on this side of the river."

"Copy," said Nate. "I'm still 20 or 30 minutes away."

The warden guided the truck across the bridge and followed the driveway across a cattle guard and into a grassy yard. She stopped 150 feet from the home in front of the garage. The home was small, perhaps only two bedrooms, and was likely the original ranch home for this property. The ranch owner had probably given into his wife's desire to live in town, so after a few good years when beef prices were high, he sold the original house and five acres to someone who wanted to live in semi-isolation. Then he and his wife built a large home in town and regretted living out of earshot of running water for the rest of their lives.

The old garage looked like it might last another winter before it collapsed. Two or three abandoned pickup trucks poked out from behind the garage, and a barn sat between the house and the river.

Daisey Mae turned to Caleb and said with a cautionary tone, "This is going to be interesting. I know the woman who lives in this house. She used to work for me. I'm not sure if she'll be much help." Then she added in a stern voice, "You, my friend, are going to have to stay in the truck no matter what. Keep your eyes peeled for anything. Tap on the horn if you see anything important, okay?"

Caleb agreed. As the warden stepped out of the truck and closed the door, he sighed and thought how lucky he was to be playing high stakes hide-and-seek with a real escaped prisoner, a former Marine sergeant turned prison warden, and Deputy Nate Garner and his wonder-dog Boo.

# CHAPTER 8

From out of nowhere, a pack of ranch yard mutts emerged who were all bark and no bite. Seven dogs of various sizes and mixes of breeds surrounded Daisey Mae, each announcing they would defend their territory to the death with a disorganized chorus of barks and yelps. Daisey Mae knew to ignore the blustering gang and act as if she belonged. A pack of dogs like that would smell fear and leverage it. The best strategy was to respect them but just not take them very seriously.

She sauntered up to the porch, and as soon as she put one foot on the steps, the dog pack went back to their previous activities somewhere in the back of the barn. On the porch, she rang the doorbell and took two steps back. She was sure the occupant was home because she could see the pickup truck in the garage. She was also sure the occupant had heard her arrival given the noise the howling herd had produced. But she wasn't sure the occupant would come to the door. They had a history.

So, she stood back and faced the door and waited. Much to her surprise, the door opened, and she stood face-to-face with the former prison guard who lived at the end of the road in the only ranch house on the east side of the river. She didn't turn to look, but she could hear the slight sound as Caleb rolled down the window on the driver's side of the truck. He was staying put as she asked, but she hadn't said he couldn't listen to the exchange.

"Hello, Daisey Mae," the woman said.

"Hello, Roberta," the warden said. "Thank you for coming to the door."

"I hope you understand if I don't let you in," the woman said. "The last time we talked, it didn't go very well for me."

"I understand," said Daisey Mae.

The conversation was moving at a slow and deliberate pace. There was caution, but no open hostility.

"I was wondering if you could help us," Daisey Mae said carefully.

"I'm not sure I'm willing to help someone who fired me for something I didn't do," said Roberta.

Daisey Mae continued with her request, sidestepping the issue that would have been the elephant in the room if they'd been standing in a room. "You might remember Kwayah." She deliberately used the runner's Indian name because she knew the former guard had been friends with the girl.

Roberta nodded. Daisey Mae continued, "Last night she made a rope from sheets, cut through the old window, and lowered herself onto the grass. Then she started running."

"Oh." Then in a sarcastic tone Roberta said, "If I had to put up with the abuse of the night shift, I would run too." Daisey Mae sidestepped that barb too and continued. "She only has a few months before being released. She has good family support. She's a model prisoner and a good person, and I want to find her before this turns into a bigger deal than it needs to be."

Roberta stared at the warden. In the awkward silence, she finally said, "So what brings you here?"

"Her tracks," the warden said directly and for effect. "We tracked her to the bridge and to your front gate."

There was another awkward pause.

"Is she here?"

Again, more silence. Roberta looked at the ground. Then she cleared her throat and responded,

"I'm not sure I'm going to let you ruin another life like you ruined mine." She looked up at the warden, the glint in her eye making it clear she hoped her words had hit home.

Daisey looked down at her feet in discomfort. "I don't need to tell you it will start raining crap if the law enforcement people who are right behind me start thinking you're protecting an escaped prisoner. I don't want that. And I don't want it for Kwayah either. So, let's try to work this out."

Roberta folded her arms. She was a muscular, hard-working woman with streaks of gray in her hair. "Work what out? My former boss who fired me from a job I loved shows up at my home and starts threatening me about a former prisoner who I tried to protect."

Daisey Mae motioned to the porch furniture, Roberta nodded, and the two sat down, facing each other. As they talked for the next five minutes, their voices rose and fell. Sometimes arms were folded or hands were waved, but all the time there seemed to be a willingness to keep the conversation going.

Finally, Daisey Mae looked over at the pickup truck and caught Caleb's eye. Then she motioned for him to come to the porch. Caleb slid out of the truck on the driver's side and walked across the gravel driveway to the porch steps.

"Roberta," the warden said, "this is Deputy Caleb…. Oh, sorry, what's your last name?" The introduction had the desired effect, and Roberta cracked a smile.

"Caleb assists Deputy Nate Garner from Lincoln County. He's that not so famous deputy with the famous dog. Nate and Boo are probably trying to make it over those barbed wire fences on the northwest side of the river right about now." There was another smile. Not a laugh. But just a smile. The ice had broken just a little bit, and Roberta was willing to listen.

Roberta looked at Caleb and said, "You like dogs?" He nodded. But before he could say anything, she said, "So do I. I've got a pack of pound hounds that you met."

Caleb settled on the porch step where he could hear the two women continue to "work it out." Down the road about a quarter of a mile, Nate and Boo were on the other side of the river heading towards the bridge and the ranch house.

"Roberta," Daisey Mae said, firmly but kindly, "I'm willing to take a second look at this. If I knew then what I know now, I wouldn't have believed Gare and her cronies at the time. I guess I was naïve, but I didn't think they would lie so convincingly."

Roberta said nothing, but the warden could see on her face that she was relaxing.

"I can't promise you your job back," the warden continued. "Human Resources might freak out, and you certainly would experience retaliation. I certainly did when I blew the whistle in Rawlins. I was right about everything, and my reward was to leave. It just wasn't safe for me to be in a prison where I was the one to temporarily cut off their drug supply. The good news for me was that they sent me to Evanston and gave me a chance to create a better kind of prison."

"I'm not sure I want to come back to work," said Roberta. "I miss the women. I miss helping those like Kwayah who had a chance of making a better life. But I don't miss the politics of that crazy organization or the guards who think that just because they have a khaki shirt and a badge that they're a 'good guy.'"

Both women nodded agreement. Roberta continued, "When that Lincoln County Sheriff's pickup pulled up in my yard, I didn't know what to think. But when I saw you get out, I thought we'd have a nice shouting match on my front porch. I'm glad you listened, Daisey Mae. I'm glad you let me tell my story."

Daisey Mae reached out her hand, and so did Roberta, and the two shook hands.

"Where is she?" Daisey Mae asked.

"I don't know," Roberta said, deflating any progress made in the conversation.

"Was she here?" the warden rephrased the question. Roberta waited, then looked over at Caleb. Daisey Mae didn't follow her gaze, but she had deliberately brought him into the space of the difficult conversation because adults were more likely to act like adults when children were around.

"I'm not sure if I should say anything," Roberta said under her breath.

"Did she come to your house? Did you feed her? Did she tell you where she was going?" Daisey Mae was exasperated.

"Oh, I know where she's going."

"Where?"

"Home."

The warden let out a sigh. "I need to catch her before the whole state is looking for her. Before the Gare posse rides out. Before some well-meaning citizen with a gun thinks he's doing the world a favor by taking her out. Help me here. Please."

"I don't know who to help," said Roberta.

As she finished the sentence, Nate came over the bridge and into the yard. He immediately loaded Boo into the cab of the truck, anticipating the dog mob greeting that was on its way. Sure enough, the hoard of self-important canines sensed a visitor and, with a divide and conquer strategy, emerged from behind the barn. Half of the critters circled Nate while the others circled the truck. Boo just sat calmly ignoring animals he considered to be lesser than his pedigree.

Roberta offered the dogs a hollow scolding in a high voice, but the words were ignored by the pack. They were offered more for the visitors to hear because inaction might be seen as agreement.

When the noise subsided, the pounding paws returned to the unknown distraction behind the barn, and Daisey Mae motioned for Nate to join the two women on the porch. As he passed Caleb on the steps, he put his hand on his shoulder, acknowledging that they were on the same team.

"Nate, this is Roberta." The warden spoke in a formal tone. "She and I used to work together." The two shook hands then Nate settled into an open chair.

After a moment, he took the direct approach. "Where is the runner?" he said, looking around.

"She's not here," Roberta said with certainty.

"How do you know that?" Nate was direct.

"I'm not going to say," Roberta said. Nate looked over at Daisey Mae and got nonverbal permission to continue.

"But you know about her, so you must have had contact with her." There was silence.

"Do we need a search warrant?" he asked.

"You can look everywhere, but she's not here." There was a long silence, then Roberta said, "You're not going to catch her."

"Yes, we will," Nate said with confidence. "It's just a matter of an easy catch or a prolonged catch. But we will catch her. I know she's around here…"

Boo started bouncing around the cab of the truck. He stuck his nose out the crack in the passenger window then began moving from the front seat to the back seat in a nervous pattern. Instinctively, Caleb rose and walked towards the truck to see what was making the dog squirm. As he did, the adults saw his head suddenly shift while he appeared to take a few seconds to focus on the hill above the house. Then his mouth flew open.

"Look!" He pointed at the ridge 300 feet above the backyard of the house. The three adults ran over to the truck. The silhouette of a runner was visible a half mile away, but with the binoculars they could see she was no longer wearing prisoner garb. She had long, nylon running pants, a small hydration pack, shoes, and a jacket. After just a few seconds, she dropped over the ridge and out of sight.

Daisey Mae looked at Roberta with disappointment. "You knew all along," she said. "I would have been better off–"

"You're not going to catch her," Roberta interrupted.

"We have to," said the warden.

# CHAPTER 9

Caleb could feel the ground shaking. The vibrating rails signaled the oncoming train that they felt before they saw. Caleb called Boo to his side and held him around his chest for security. He knew the noise of a passing train would be stressful for the dog. Then he looked over and saw Nate motioning for him to join them in the safety of the truck.

Two hours earlier, Warden Daisey Mae Cromwell, Deputy Nate Garner, thirteen-year-old Caleb, and Boo the-wonder-dog had watched as the escaped prisoner they were pursuing climbed over a ridge above a ranch and disappeared towards the Union Pacific Railroad line. Nate had immediately taken out his map and charted the direction of travel of the runner, and the line intersected the Transcontinental Main Line of the Union Pacific just two miles away.

"She's probably going to try to jump on a train," Nate said.

Daisey Mae agreed. "That would be the easiest way to get east towards Fort Washakie."

"I doubt she'll be able to catch a moving train," Caleb chimed in. "She's a fast runner but not that fast."

"I think the trains slow down before they enter the tunnel," said Daisey Mae. "Maybe she's going to try to hop on when the train slows near the entrance."

So, with Nate driving, the search team took twenty miles of dirt and gravel roads around the hills and ranches to go two miles as-the-crow-flies to the railroad tracks. With permission from the Union Pacific security officers, they pulled onto the service road that paralleled the tracks. When Nate stopped to rest, Caleb was giving the assignment to put the dog back on the track command and see if he could find the runner.

"Will the fact that she took off her prison garb and put on all new clothes at Roberta's make it harder for the dog?" Daisey Mae asked.

"No," said Nate. "The dog is following the dead skin cells that slough off her body. They have a distinct scent and really can't be masked."

"It's kind of amazing," added Caleb. "We're all creating a trail of dead skin cells all the time, and Boo can smell them."

"He knows through his nose," said Nate, grinning at Caleb. He had said that same line a thousand times while explaining the talents of his exceptionally gifted canine.

Boo and Caleb stepped out of the truck, and before Caleb could put him on command, he crossed over the tracks and immediately put his nose to the ground and began following along the path that paralleled the tracks. In a half-hearted voice, Caleb commanded him to "track," but Boo was already doing that.

"How does he know which way to go?" Daisey Mae asked the deputy as he navigated the service road and followed at the speed of the tracking dog.

"Dogs are descendants of wolves. Generations ago, they developed the ability to follow a scent trail to their next meal, but they can also tell the age of the trail down to the minute. If they go the wrong direction, the trail scent gets older. If they go the right direction, the trail scent gets newer."

"It's amazing to watch." Daisey Mae said.

"It's still amazing for me to watch," Nate said honestly. "And I've been watching for a lot of years."

The two rode along in silence for a few minutes, watching Boo lead Caleb on the other side of the tracks. Then they heard the noise of the oncoming train and saw Caleb pull the dog close. When Caleb looked over at Nate, he motioned for the boy and the dog to cross back over to the truck. Just as they piled into the truck, a massive diesel locomotive with two helper engines came around the bend going westbound. Seeing the truck, the engineers pulled on the deafening horn that Caleb thought was loud enough to crack the windshield on the truck. He was glad Boo was in the protective cab of the truck because his sensitive ears would have been overpowered by a direct shot from the horn.

The train was pulling flat cars with shipping containers that had been loaded in China, offloaded in Long Beach, and were destined for the Midwest or southern US. This was the main line of the Union Pacific Railroad, the same line that had been functioning since 1869 when it was inaugurated as the first transcontinental railroad.

Efforts to connect the coasts of the United States began in 1863 with the formation of two competing companies. The Central Pacific Railroad started in Sacramento, California, and began building east, crossing the Sierra Nevada range and what was now Nevada. The Union Pacific Railroad began in Council Bluffs, Iowa, along the Mississippi River, and crossed the central US into Wyoming. On May 10, 1869, they connected at Promontory Point, Utah. The Central Pacific had laid 690 miles of track, and the Union Pacific had laid 1087 miles of track. The original hand-dug track bed was still visible from the current track that bore thousands of trains a year, including Amtrak passenger trains.

Before the mile-long eastbound train had passed, a westbound train came up from behind on the parallel track and also offered it's horn at full blast. Having two massive trains moving on tracks just a stone's throw away was not only deafening, but it also caused the whole truck to vibrate.

"Look," the warden said over the multi-pitched sounds of metal on metal. "The eastbound train is slowing down."

"I think the tunnel is just around the bend." Nate yelled. "Maybe we're too late."

"I know the railroad police will be looking for her," Daisey Mae said in a loud voice, trying to overcome the screeching wheels of the trains. "But I have the naïve hope we could catch her before they did."

"I don't think that's going to happen," Nate said.

Nate crawled the pickup truck along the service road. As the little valley opened up, they could see two tunnels. One was down and to the right. It was called the Aspen Tunnel. The other was up and to the right. It was labeled the Altamont Tunnel. The last car on the westbound train was just coming out of the Aspen Tunnel. Caleb had stopped counting the cars after a couple hundred passed. They all turned their attention to the slowing eastbound train that now had its head in the other tunnel. Caleb thought it looked like a giant snake with its head in the ground and its body trying to follow. Nate paused the truck where they could see the right side of the train, and they watched for anyone who might be trying to hop on. Despite what old movies portrayed, hopping a train while it was moving was difficult and dangerous. You had to run the speed of the train then use your upper body strength to pull yourself three or four feet off the ground and onto a train that was designed for hauling freight not human riders.

They saw no one trying to get on the slowing train, but in the big open space, they could see a lone Union Pacific security guard looking back at them from the mouth of the tunnel. After a few minutes, the head of the giant snake had pulled its entire body into the hole, and the train was gone. The absence of noise and vibrations made the world suddenly feel silent and peaceful, Caleb thought.

Nate clipped a lead on Boo, and the three searchers and the dog exited the truck and began walking towards the tunnel. If railroads were the life blood of the American economy, then this rail line through Evanston and across Wyoming was the aorta. It carried freight, passengers, fuel, food, and farm supplies right down the center of the country. So, Caleb was shocked to see that the Aspen Tunnel had a completion date of 1902. It was well over a hundred years old, yet it was still a critical part of this essential transportation system.

In 1899, the Union Pacific began work on the tunnel which cut ten miles off the east-west journey across the United States. Just under two miles underground saved ten miles above ground. Not really worth it except that every day ten, twenty, even more trains could have a shorter journey. Within a matter of years, the tunnel had paid for itself. In fact, by 1930, the Union Pacific had built a second tunnel called the Altamont Tunnel because the single-track Aspen Tunnel had become a bottle neck.

The Union Pacific security guard walked towards the group while Boo twisted his nose, trying to get around the low-level toxicity of the creosol and diesel smells. As soon as they were within shouting range, the guard spoke up.

No doubt this was the most exciting thing that had happened for the security guard for months. "I didn't see anyone trying to hop that train," he said before introductions or pleasantries were exchanged. "I had the train crew watching carefully on the other side, and they didn't see nothin'." The security guard looked to be in his sixties and was a good pair of eyes. He had an equipment belt around his bulging waist that held handcuffs, a gun, a taser, and a big handheld radio, and he wore an official-looking uniform. But he was not up to the physical task of stopping a subject or making an arrest.

"Thanks for helping us out," Daisey Mae said.

"No problem. Glad to help." He took out his radio and spoke a few words into the mike, presumably to the train crew that had just passed. Then he focused on the trio with the dog before him.

"How often do you get eastbound trains?" Daisey Mae asked.

"Oh, about every hour. Sometimes more often than that. The previous train was twenty minutes ago, but we had eyes on that one, and I doubt she was on board." Then he turned and looked at Nate. "You from Lincoln County?"

"Yup." Like most men in Wyoming, Nate seemed to believe he might run out of words if he used too many of them.

"I worked as a deputy in Lincoln in the sixties and seventies." The security guard was trying to enter the social space. The inevitable "do you know" question was coming next. It always did. The population of Wyoming was small enough that most people knew most people. And if they didn't, they knew someone who knew someone who knew the friend. Rather than six degrees of separation, it was two or three degrees.

"Do you know Kathy McConkie?"

"I think everyone knows Kathy," Nate said.

Not wanting this to turn into a social conversation, Daisey Mae intervened and asked, "If our fugitive is on a train, we missed her. Could we run the dog around this area and see if she has been here?"

"Oh, he's already on that," Caleb said. He was holding the lead, and Boo was pulling him towards the far tracks and the far tunnel. With the permission of the security guard, they crossed the tracks used by the eastbound train and headed towards the second tunnel used by the westbound train.

"I don't understand," said Daisey Mae. "A westbound train just takes her back to Evanston then down Echo Canyon and into Ogden, Utah. Her people are east not west."

"Let's see what Boo tells us," Nate said. Boo went nose down on the far side of the second track, indicating he was finding a familiar scent. There was garbage, and the rocks were covered with a brown oily substance that came from constant exposure to diesel exhaust. But none of this interfered with his ability to find her track and set a direction.

The dog paralleled the tracks. Then just before they entered into the tunnel, he followed the scent up the side of the hill.

"Now that makes no sense at all," Daisey Mae said. "She's headed east. She's not on a train. And it looks like she's walking. I'll bet she's trying to confuse us."

Frustrated, Daisey Mae said, "I think we should look in the tunnel. Maybe she's hiding inside it."

The Union Pacific security guard had caught up with the trio, and he volunteered to go into the tunnel "for a quick look because the next train would not arrive for fifteen minutes." He walked into the black, pulling a massive flashlight off his utility belt as he disappeared.

To add to her frustration, Daisey Mae's phone kept buzzing. Finally, she received a call linked to an unusual ring tone. Caleb gathered it was her boss and it was urgent. She opened the device, turned her back on

Nate and Caleb, and began slowly walking away. Caleb could hear only part of the conversation.

"No, we have not recaptured her. … Yes, we have made progress. … No, I have not been able to fully question all the guards. … Yes, I will be back there tonight." Daisey Mae hung up the cellphone and said, "This search is over for me. My boss in Rawlins says I need to go back to being a prison warden. He says the night crew is already spinning the rumor mill about what happened to make her run."

"We're pretty much done for the day too," said Nate. "The dog is spent, and we're losing daylight. It would be best if we took a break and got on this first thing in the morning."

Caleb knew that "first thing in the morning" for Nate meant very, very early. Maybe up at four a.m. and out as soon as they put their pants on. He was glad Nate was a big breakfast eater. That would at least give him something to look forward to.

Meanwhile, Boo had continued up the steep side of the hill over the tunnel and was now tracking with confidence. "I think we can pick that up in the morning," Nate said. Then he turned and walked with Daisey Mae towards the pickup truck. Caleb called Boo, who ignored the first "come" command. Tired as the dog was, he wanted to keep tracking. But he did come reluctantly on the second call, surveying the humans as if they were quitters. If he could talk, Caleb imagined he would be saying, "Hey, the party isn't over yet."

# CHAPTER 10

From the front of the dusty half-mile procession, Brother and Sister Larson looked across the sagebrush over the string of weary walkers pulling the pioneer handcarts. The mostly youthful walkers were barely able to lift their legs or move their feet, yet they kept moving forward. In her mind first, then on her lips, she quietly hummed the tune and whispered the lyrics of the pioneer song she sang as a child. "Some will push, and some will pull as we go walking up the hill, and merrily on the way we go until we reach the valley, oh."

There was nothing merry about this group. They missed their cell phones and video games. They wanted nylon, breathable clothing instead of sweat absorbing cotton. They were hungry, in some cases hangry. They were worried about where they would sleep and what they would sleep in. Some were pushing. And some were pulling. And some were just stumbling along. One young woman was riding in the back of a handcart, plopped down over the canvas bundles like another piece of cargo.

The procession was identical in look to the Mormon Handcart Companies that crossed the plains in the 1850s and 1860s, before the transcontinental railroad, except for two things. First, with the exception of adult leaders like Shelby and Jay Larson, they were young. Mostly between fourteen and eighteen years old. Second, while they were wearing authentic pioneer clothing and hats, they could wear whatever footwear they thought comfortable.

This was a fall break reenactment designed to help these young members of the Church of Jesus Christ of Latter-day Saints appreciate their pioneer ancestors. It was not working. Even though they were asked to make this a realistic experience, most of the youth had smuggled in snacks to supplement the basic but generous pioneer menu. That was actually a third difference—unlike with the pioneers, food would be plentiful, and no one would risk starvation. Biscuits and all-you-can-eat stew, which would have been luxury food for pioneers, was not appreciated by the group, except for a small number of teenage boys who valued food quantity over quality.

The youth and their adult supporters had left their homes in Salt Lake City the day before on this adventure that actually followed parts of the Mormon Trail in Wyoming. The campsites had been well used throughout the summer, and the handcarts and guiding services were provided by a group of enterprising Wyoming riders who had found a safe way to earn cash money to supplement their hobby of raising cows in this unforgiving country. One rider was stationed at the front of the long line of about fifty church youth and another at the end.

He certainly was not like a real pioneer, but Jay Larson had a handheld radio concealed in his pants pocket that he could use to call either of the cowboys in case of an emergency. Actually, he could call them in case of an inconvenience, and they would ride up and help, particularly if the person needing help was a cute sixteen-year-old city girl.

The first twenty-four hours of the experience had been very realistic, though they could hear the Union Pacific Railroad trains entering and exciting the tunnel several draws over. From the high point, they could also see the cars on the transcontinental ribbon of asphalt called I-80 about ten miles away. But still many of the young people were having just enough of a challenge, becoming pliable, teachable, and even curious about the past.

The lead cowboy arrived at a large flat meadow overlooking the sage prairie flats and called, "Circle up." As the lead handcarts came into camp, they began to form a circle. A single campfire would be placed in the center where they would cook stew, biscuits, and cobbler in Dutch ovens. The cowboy guides had already gathered wood for the fires and prepared them when they came through on their ATVs earlier in the week. Before all the stragglers wandered into camp, the fires were burning high. Soon the coals would be ready for cooking.

The youth were reenacting the Mormon migration from Nauvoo, Illinois, to the valley of the Great Salt Lake that began in 1847 when mobs in Ohio and Illinois burned the homes of the people who called themselves "Latter-day Saints." For the next twenty years, over 250 companies of pioneers followed the Oregon Trail to Fort Bridger, Wyoming, then turned south on the Mormon Trail to join Brigham Young in Salt Lake also known as Zion. All but ten of the companies were ox or horse-driven. But those ten companies, the immigrants were too poor to have livestock, so they pulled their belongings, limited to seventeen pounds, in an oversized wheelbarrow called a handcart.

The most famous of these ten companies were the Martin and Willie Handcart Companies. Every Latter-day Saint youth had heard the story of the almost one thousand handcart pioneers who had left what was present-day Omaha, Nebraska, late in the season. Church missionary Levi Savage warned them to wait until the next year because they couldn't travel "with a mixed company of aged people, women, and little children so late in the season without much suffering, sickness, and death." But the attraction of the migration to Zion was too strong. One in five would die in an early winter storm or freeze to death crossing a river. Eventually, Brigham Young sent a rescue mission from Salt Lake, and when they succeeded, the survivors and rescuers became legends.

On this night, the city-raised descendants of pioneers felt like anything but a legend. They had only covered seven miles that day, half the distance of a real pioneer. But their feet were covered with blisters, and their brows were sunburned, even though it was mid-October and the fall chill was ever present. The youth and their leaders naturally gravitated towards the fire, not so much for the warmth as for the company. They could already smell the aroma of the stew, and while it was not the food of their favorite fast-food restaurant, it was hot and filling for their hollow stomachs.

As the sun set, the firelight danced on the hills surrounding the hollow meadow. In almost perfect timing, the near full moon rose, and a light breeze ruffled the sagebrush. Before long, each of the youth had found a seat on a blanket or log near the fire and had a large serving of stew on their tin plate. The cowboys and the youth leaders acted as servers, and the youth were already testing out their stories on each other.

"I think I saw a rattlesnake."

"I would die for just two minutes on my cell phone."

"I would die if I walked another fifty feet."

"I wish I could ride on the back of that cowboy's horse."

As the bellies filled and the food kept coming, the crowd quieted down. Jay Larsen asked one of the youth to offer a prayer, which he did. Then another led the group in an old Mormon hymn. The voices were tired, and the chorus was unrehearsed, but the tune was sincere, and several of the young women teared up as they softly sang:

*Come, come, ye Saints, no toil nor labor fear*
*But with joy wend your way*
*Though hard to you this journey may appear*
*Grace shall be as your day.*
*Gird up your loins, fresh courage take*
*Our God will never us forsake*
*And soon we'll have this tale to tell*
*All is well! All is well!*
*We'll find the place which God for us prepared*
*Far away in the West*
*Where none shall come to hurt or make afraid*
*There the Saints will be blessed.*

The fire was turning to coals, and the hearts of the young people had turned to their great-grandfathers and grandmothers who might have walked these paths not knowing what was before them. Jay and Shelby stood in the shadows and found just the right words to make the moment unforgettable. Then it was the cowboys' turn. Their presentation was less reverent but equally appreciated. Their well-rehearsed campfire stories, with a song, were designed to put the youth to sleep but not make them sleep too well. As they poked fun at sheepherders, talked about wild bears and wolves, their embellished prose quieted the crowd, and before long, the group found themselves with an arm around a friend or a hand interlaced with a neighbor.

In the perfect moment, just beyond the light of the dying fire, a figure emerged. A stranger. An unknown girl, maybe a woman, who had been drawn by the hymn. It was hard to know how long she had been there, but as she stepped into the firelight, the cowboys' horses whinnied in the distance. She had long, beautiful black hair and deep hazel eyes that danced with the coals in the fire. She was dressed in modern clothing, with running shoes, sweatpants, a jacket, and a small pack. She was small in stature but stood erect and confident with her thumb looped in the strap of her pack. In her dramatic presentation, they could see she was tired, perhaps more tired than the city youth who had done something very hard for them.

Sister Larsen stood up and opened her arms then took three steps towards the stranger. Before the youth leader could open her mouth, the mystery woman answered the question they were all thinking. She said, "These were once the lands of my people. My name is Kwayah. I am the North Wind. Will you share your food?"

# CHAPTER 11

Caleb stirred the ashes of the fire as he watched the young people his age and older pack their handcarts and prepare for another day of trekking. For Caleb, it looked like fun. But some of the trekkers who were city kids looked at him with envy. It appeared they would rather be going to jail in a sheriff's pickup truck than pulling a handcart. Caleb imagined that was not unlike the real pioneers. Some were comfortable in the wild. But for most, every step balanced fear and faith. When fear won, they would turn around and go back to the edge of civilization. When faith would win, they moved forward, at least for the next day.

Nate was speaking with a middle-aged woman who stood facing him with folded arms in a defensive stance, resisting his inquiry. Caleb was holding Boo's lead close enough to hear the conversation but far enough away that the woman called Sister Larsen assumed he could not.

"At first, we weren't sure if it was part of the campfire program," she said. "The wranglers said they would have a surprise for the campfire program. So, I thought she was their surprise."

"They said they thought she was part of your program," Nate interjected.

"Well, she was a surprise," Shelby said. "We thought it was just a story until someone offered her a bowl of stew and she devoured it in three bites and asked for seconds. People playing a role at a campfire aren't that good at acting. She really wolfed down the food…"

"So where is she now?" Nate asked, cutting the woman off.

Shelby looked at Nate then at Caleb. Boo was lying at Caleb's feet, and on cue, he walked slowly over to Sister Larsen and looked directly into her face. Then he pushed his nose into her thigh and asked for affection. As the woman scratched the loving dog's ears, she said, "You're not going to catch her."

"We have to," said Nate. "Do you know where she's going?"

"She's going home. To her people. To her child."

"Her home is northeast on the Shoshone Reservation, but she's headed southeast. We thought she'd hop a train to get home quickly, but now she's wandering around. I don't think it's safe for her."

"You don't know her!" Sister Larsen interjected. Nate felt chastised. Then the well-meaning woman said, "We stayed up most of the night talking. She told me everything. I mean everything. I know she's going home. But home is not north. Home is not Fort Washakie. That was her husband's home. Her home is south. Home is Fort Duchesne and White Rock."

Nate was stunned. He was not sure what that meant.

"My sister is Ute. She is not Shoshone. She is headed home across the Uintah Mountains," the mild woman said with as much authority as she could muster. Then she added, "You will not catch her."

The line of pioneer wannabees stretched out a quarter of a mile now, twisting up a gradual incline to a ridge. A young woman with dark hair led the procession. She was dressed in a loose-fitting pioneer dress. She had a strong gait and was moving faster than the others, gaining speed as she hiked up the trail and neared the ridge. Nate took the binoculars and focused on the woman. Without slowing down, she pulled off her bonnet, unbuttoned her dress and pulled it over her head in one motion, placing it on a nearby rock. Underneath was the runner now clad in her black nylon warm ups.

The wrangler rode up to her on his tall horse used for pushing cows. He handed her a plastic water bottle, which she drained. Then he gave her a small pack and pivoted his horse like a rodeo cowboy. As he did, the youth stopped their slow climb up the hill and began to clap. The runner waved at the procession, and the claps turned to chants. "Go. Go. Go," they chanted as she began her effortless steady pace to the top of the ridge. Amazed at what they were seeing, Nate and Caleb stood with their feet frozen in place until the runner reached the high point on the ridge. There she turned south and followed the flat of the ridge for a few hundred feet before disappearing over the other side.

# CHAPTER 12

"Jump in!"

Caleb had anticipated the urgency and already had one leg up into the cab of the pickup and was buckling his seat belt. He called the dog who vaulted in one motion into the back row of the cab and settled in his favorite place behind Nate. Nate put his foot on the brake as he stepped into the cab, turning the key in the same motion. He flipped the switch and turned on his red and blue wig wag lights out of habit. He did that whenever he was in a hurry, though no one was there to see them and get out of the way. A few stragglers heading up to the ridge in their handcarts turned around in surprise. He revved the engine, dropped the sheriff's pickup into gear, and pointed the truck back towards civilization. It was a high-speed chase between a runner and a high clearance vehicle on a rutted road.

"She's headed south. With help, we'll be able to trap her at the Sulphur Creek Reservoir," Nate explained to an excited Caleb. The Sulphur Creek Dam provided a perfect pinch point where the road from Evanston came around the dam. Cliffs populated the uphill side, and a steep drop-off into the water dominated the other. Nate crawled the pickup past the second wrangler who was bringing up the rear of the handcart procession then bounced over a washed-out part of the road, trying carefully not to break an axle or scratch the door panel on a bush or rock. It was more of the same for the next three miles. The road, if you could call it that, prevented Nate from anything over five miles an hour. That was slower than the escapee was running, and she had a more direct route.

Dust coated the hood of the truck as it rocked back and forth down the rutted road. The radio and other equipment rattled, and pens, a lunch box, and other small items flew about. Boo climbed into the foot space between the front and back seats. It was his safe place. Caleb just braced himself, holding the handle over the door. As the deputy carefully guided the vehicle down the remnants of the "Mormon Trail," he tried calling Daisey Mae. When she didn't answer, he called the sheriff who had originally called him to this case.

Over the rattling din, Nate said, "Hey, Rondo! This is Nate. I'm hot on her tail. She just went over a ridge and is headed south towards Sulphur Creek Reservoir. Can you come help?"

Pause.

"If you come in from the west and I come in from the east, we can trap her along the shore."

Caleb couldn't hear the other part of the conversation, but he could hear Nate's adrenaline-fueled voice.

"Yes, she's running, and hard. She doesn't want to get caught."

Another pause.

"Hey, some interesting background. Turns out she's Ute. Not Shoshone. Looks like the information we were given was wrong. She shared her story with a group of handcart reenactors who shared it with me. It's a long story, but she married a Shoshone boy she met in a high school track meet and moved to the Shoshone reservation, but her people are Ute. Apparently, she's a track superstar and was recruited by all the big universities out of high school. Instead, she got married to this boy in Wyoming, probably because she was pregnant. He turned out to be a meth head and a dealer. He ran away then later died of a staged overdose last year. Shortly after that, his drug supplier came collecting at her front door, the same guy who was with her husband when he died. He who accused her of assault. She pled guilty under pressure from he lawyer, and that's why she's in jail."

Nate nodded his head to something Caleb couldn't hear. "Right. It's a mess. I've got to drive, but there's a lot more to this story than I had imagined. The bottom line is she's headed south toward Fort Duchesne in Utah not north to Fort Washakie in Wyoming. It looks to me like she's going to try to cross the High Uintahs Wilderness."

There were more unheard comments from the sheriff.

"I know. It's already almost winter in that part of the world. But you need to watch this woman run. She could easily cover thirty miles in a day. Daisey Mae said she wore out the prison treadmill."

Nate paused, listening.

"The way she's headed, she'll come out somewhere on the north side of Sulphur Creek. If you can position your car with lights flashing at the dam, then I'll come into the boat launch and campground and try to make contact with her. I think we can talk her into surrendering."

Caleb could hear a voice of disagreement on the other end of the line as Nate listened. Then he said, "Trust me on this one, Rondo. She spoke at a campfire with a bunch of Mormon kids last night. Made a big impression. She's not dangerous. She's just driven. I think it's only the drug dealers she doesn't like."

There was more from the unheard sheriff then Nate concluded. "Yes, I'll work towards you through the campground. But hold your position on the dam."

Nate hung up the phone and focused on driving. "Okay, Caleb, in a few minutes, we're going to intercept a two-lane gravel road that will follow the old Union Pacific Railroad bed that was used before the tunnels were built. That road will loop around the hills and take us to the north side of Sulphur Creek Reservoir."

"Is that where you hope to cut her off?"

"That's the plan. She's coming from the north, and she won't be able to go south because of the water or west because Rondo will be blocking the road. So, we'll come in from the east, get close, and try to convince her peacefully to return to prison."

Caleb's head bounced lightly against the side window as they came to the end of the single-track spur and tractioned up onto a real gavel road that, in contrast to what they'd been experiencing, felt like a smooth freeway.

"What the...heck?" Nate glanced over, and Caleb hid his smile knowing his friend had curbed the language for his sake. He also knew Nate didn't want to contribute to the profanity jar Marie kept on their mantle. But the reason for his exclamation was just ahead. Two vehicles could be seen near the intersection between the Mormon Trail and the two-lane gravel road. With the exception of the wooden, large-wheeled handcarts, they hadn't seen a vehicle all day. Now they had come across what appeared to be a Wyoming rush hour traffic jam. Their eyes fell first on a black Jeep Rubicon decked out with all the off-road features, including tinted windows, a light rack on top, external fuel tanks on the sides, and tools for getting unstuck attached to a full-sized spare tire on the back.

"That's odd," Nate said.

"What is it?"

"Well, it's my police training kicking in, but do you notice something unusual about that vehicle?"

Caleb stared at it for just a moment. "Well, it's an off-road vehicle, but it looks really clean."

"Bingo. I only see a little dust in the wheel wells. I'm guessing it has never been driven off road, but it looks instead like it's a statement of dominance. Also, the Wyoming license plate says it's from Fremont County. What would bring a person from Freemont County to this back road in Uintah County? I know Fort Washakie is in Fremont County."

The second vehicle was a typical older model Wyoming pickup truck. It had once been the work horse on a ranch but now in its declining years had patches of rust between patches of dust. The tires didn't match, and the door panel had been salvaged from a similar model, different color junked car but never painted. "You see that other truck? I've seen it before."

"Me too! It was in the prison parking lot, wasn't it?"

"Good catch. I saw it when I watched the night shift prison guards leave yesterday. It's one of their vehicles."

Nate slowed way down. The two vehicles were parked nose-to-nose in the right lane of the road. A short Native American was standing between the cars, and two white men were watching as he pointed to something on a map that was spread out on the hood of the Jeep. The Native American man had dark sunglasses and a black shirt. He wore black pants and black leather cowboy boots with silver pointed tips. The boots were polished. And so was the turquoise pendant that hung around his neck. The white men wore T-shirts and weathered jeans. Their cowboy boots were scuffed and worn from use in the corral and barn.

Nate looked over at Caleb and gave him a cautionary glance. Realizing that his wig wag lights were still on, he flipped them off. "It's unusual for people to use a map," he whispered to Caleb as he pulled alongside the men.

"Can I help you gentlemen find something?" Nate asked in his professional cop voice.

"Thank you, officer," the man in the sunglasses said while the two white men turned their faces away.

"We're just scouting some wildlife." Caleb could see the vague excuse quickly offered made Nate even more nervous and suspicious. Boo picked up on his concern and jumped up on the passenger seat just in time to focus on the trio as they passed by. It was unusual for him to growl. But he did, and Caleb knew something was not right about those three.

"What are they doing out here in the middle of sagebrush city?" Caleb said, giving voice to what they were both thinking.

"Something they don't what us to know about," said Nate. "It might not be illegal, but they didn't want us to stop and see what they were doing."

Nate slowly accelerated onto the gravel road. They were now traveling at forty-five miles-per-hour. Hopefully fast enough to intercept the runner at the water barrier of the reservoir.

Twenty minutes later, Nate abruptly stopped his pickup in front of the gate to the Sulphur Creek boat launch and campground. To his surprise, a large sign on the gate said, "Low Water-Closed for the Season." No cars were on the road and no boats on the lake. The gate in front of them was locked. Without waiting for him to ask, Caleb handed him the binoculars, and he took them and scanned the hills on the north side. He shook his head—nothing. Then he slowly passed the glasses down the road to the campground a mile away. "Gee, the boat launch ends a hundred feet above the low water line." He also scanned the outbuildings, picnic pavilions, and guard shack.

The radio crackled, "Nate! It's Rondo." They were on a car-to-car without being monitored by the dispatch, so professional cop talk and code talk was not required. "I think I see her."

Nate and Caleb climbed out of the truck for a better view. Nate put the binoculars on the hood and scanned with the wider angle of his eyes. Caleb followed his gaze. He could see past the campground to the dam and the flashing wig wag lights of Rondo's car blocking the road.

"Someone is in the alcove of the third outhouse, the one closest to you."

"Rondo, you've got the eyes of an elk hunter." That was the ultimate compliment for Wyoming residents. "I'm stuck behind this locked gate," Nate said. He pointed out for Caleb the public restroom that Rondo had identified. They could see nothing at first then saw a small movement behind the outside privacy panel. Nate took the binoculars again, focusing on the eighteen-inch space between the ground and the panel. "I can see her moving feet. I recognize the brightly colored shoes she got from her prison guard friend. But I can't tell what she's doing behind that panel."

Adjacent to the outhouse was a turned over trash can. The runner stepped out of her hiding place and took the liner out of the trash can then took the contents of her small pack and placed them in the garbage bag. Then she removed her shoes, her shirt, and her long running pants.

As she did, Nate put the binoculars on the hood of the car, took off his police belt with his gun and taser. With the radio in his right hand, he called Boo and stepped around the locked gate. Caleb could see the runner make eye contact with Nate, even though she was a half mile away. Then she looked over her shoulder at the police car to the west, blocking escape in that direction.

Nate began to jog towards the runner, his beautiful blond golden retriever heeling on his left side as they ran. Nate didn't need to say it—Caleb was to stay in the truck. But he didn't. He picked up the binoculars and followed Nate at a slower pace. He wanted to see this play out.

The runner could see Nate approaching but went about organizing deliberately and without haste. Caleb stopped and placed the binoculars to his face. The runner had returned to the shelter of the panels. He could see her pack on the ground and her legs moving. Nate was getting closer, and Boo had moved out front. Nate stopped and called the woman's name. Caleb couldn't hear what was being said, but he imagined reassuring words. He wasn't sure if Nate had left his gun and handcuffs behind so he could run faster or to convince the runner he was going to be kind.

When Boo was a hundred yards from the runner, and Nate was about two hundred yards, she burst out of the protection of the privacy panels and sprinted towards the lake. Caleb watched as Nate stopped with surprise then began his own sprint. But only Boo had a chance of catching her. However, he wasn't trained in the take down techniques of police dogs. He was a search and rescue dog, a tracking dog, not an aggressive police dog. So when the runner ran, the chase turned into a game for Boo.

Caleb could see she was headed towards the empty boat ramp. But he could also see something that caused him to look again. She was barefoot and bare naked. While her waist-length hair offered some privacy, the only thing she actually had on was her pack which was obviously stuffed with her shoes, running clothes, hydration pack, and whatever the pioneer trekkers had given her for food. Boo caught up with her as she reached the end of the boat ramp. His tail wafted in the light wind, and he pranced alongside her, half expecting her to treat him like Caleb did when they were training. At the end of the ramp, she continued down the gentle slope leaving distinct footprints in the surface-dried mud. She didn't break stride as she hit the water. Two splashing steps, and she dove horizontally into the water.

Nate stopped at the top of the boat ramp speechless. Then Rondo's voice crackled on the radio. "If I hadn't seen that myself, I never would have believed it."

Rondo, Caleb, and Nate, all from different angles, watched as the runner turned swimmer pulled with perfect strokes across the open water. Boo, who never passed up an opportunity to get wet, followed the runner into the water. But he couldn't keep up and turned around after a hundred yards. She covered the quarter mile of the half empty reservoir in about seven minutes, waded out of the water on the other side, and began her familiar running pace up the shoreline to a large driftwood log at the high-water mark. There she stopped and, without shame or embarrassment, removed the garbage bag from her pack, took out her clothes, and dressed. She emptied water out of the pack and placed it on her back as she stood. The runner then scanned the lake. Caleb half expected a mocking wave, but instead, she turned and ran into the trees.

Nate had no need to hurry now. The other side of the reservoir was forty-five minutes away over a dirt road. In the dense forest, she could hide, and with her tireless running, she could stay well ahead of the tracking dog. His only hope in catching her was to get ahead of her and then let her come to him. He turned and started walking back to the truck. Boo came alongside him and did a shake off, sending a light and cooling mist of water droplets around him.

Caleb was waiting at the outhouse where she had disrobed. He was puzzled. "Kinda strange," Nate said. "Daisey Mae will be disappointed that she was so afraid of us."

"It's not us," Caleb said. "It's them." He pointed back to the truck, back to the barrier that had foiled Nate's attempt to capture the runner. Next to the Lincoln County Sheriff's pickup truck was a black Jeep Rubicon and a beat up old pickup truck. As Nate looked, the three men stepped into their vehicles and drove away.

# CHAPTER 13

Thirty years with the FBI had taught Lou Bertram to fit in. He fit in working a mob undercover case in New Jersey. He fit in undercover in an embassy catching a spy. Now he fit in standing next to a trout stream trying to coax a dinner fish onto his line near his cabin in Utah. No matter where he was, he looked like he belonged. Lou had left his cabin early in the morning and hiked a mile to the East Fork of the Bear River to try out his new fly rod. Lou was a good golfer, a great hiker, and a lousy fisherman. YouTube showed him how to properly rig the fly rod. But he still couldn't figure out how to drop the fly into this small stream with the big name and let it float into a pool and make a fish take the bait. He was yet to catch a fish with his three-hundred-dollar rig that he still had not told his wife about. Thank goodness for Amazon's return policy.

But he kept trying to fly fish because just holding the rod and listening to the rippling water brought peace to his soul. For a man who had witnessed and even participated in so much violence in his life, peace was hard to come by and deeply appreciated. Unlike golf, fly fishing without success was better than any therapy. The former federal agent had spent thirty years accumulating workplace stress to the point of PTSD. It wasn't worse than any seasoned agent who had worked major cases, but it still was not easy. Sometimes at night, Lou relived the time he had shot a suspect or, worse, the time he had been shot and the bullet deflected off his body armor and into the leg of his partner.

The stream was running low. Several times, he had seen the shadow and flash of a brook trout inspecting his fly, but none had partaken of the lethal combination of feathers and metal. The fish seemed insulted by his lack of prowess with the rod, but Lou didn't take it personally. It was enough to enjoy himself in the environment he loved. Other than the black Jeep he had passed on the road, Lou hadn't seen anyone that morning. He loved the healing solitude the isolated wilderness offered. The empty trail and the open meadow were the best therapy for the aging yet fit former agent.

When Lou saw the fresh footprints of a woman, he abandoned his failed fishing expedition and was sucked into solving what he thought was a minor mystery. His man-tracking skills were rusty, but he was able to follow the eight-hour-old ground spore through the meadow. Driven by his curiosity and the fact that the fish were not biting, Lou wanted to know why a small woman with an urgent gait had also been following the steam that few people traveled. He could tell the woman weighed between 100 and 120 pounds. She was moving fast, running in most places. She also crossed the river in several places, though at this time of year it could hardly be called a river.

As Lou approached a thick collection of willows, he could see where clumps of brown fall grass had been pulled up from the meadow. It seemed strange, but the only reason he could think of that someone would gather armfuls of grass would be for bedding. At six foot four inches, Lou was eye level with the willow bushes. As he scanned over the tops of the willows, he could see the tips of one clump of bushes moving in an unnatural way. Someone was in there. It wasn't wildlife. A moose would be obvious. A bear would have smelled the human approaching and left the area long ago. Deer had already moved to the low country with the anticipation of winter. It had to be a human.

Lou had a handgun in his small backpack, along with a medical kit, some energy bars and sports drinks for survival rations, a windbreaker, and a clean pair of socks. But his cop intuition told him this was not a dangerous situation. Perhaps it was a survivalist or even a lost person. They might need help.

"Hello!" Lou hollered, not wanting to surprise whoever was fifty feet away in the thick cover. He waited then said, "I was fishing and saw your footprints. Are you okay?" Lou had learned in the FBI that most people could detect a lie. They could hear it in the tone of your voice or see it in your body language. He knew that truth was more likely to get a truthful response.

"I don't see many people in this area and just want to know if you're okay," he asked again.

There was no response, but the tops of the bushes were moving even more, and he imagined the person was dressing or putting on their shoes.

"I'm going to come in there and check on you," Lou said, surprising himself by declaring his intentions. "I want to make sure you're all right. I'm an old man, and I have no intention to harm you." His voice was friendly but firm.

The bushes stopped moving, but Lou knew exactly where to go. He had marked in his mind where the person was. He stepped into the thicket, pushing the willows away from his face and protecting his eyes. In five steps, he found himself at the center of the protective ring of willows near a large pile of meadow grass. A young woman was sitting on the grass with a mylar sleeping bag pulled around her shoulders. The tin foil like sleeping bag and the grass had clearly been her safe sleeping place during the night. Lou could see a few candy bar wrappers and a place where she had relieved herself.

"I'm sorry to enter your camp," he said in a fatherly voice. He stood at the edge of the bushes, not wanting to invade her claimed space. "I just wanted to know if you're okay." He could see she was not.

The woman was silent and appeared surprised that she had been discovered. She looked him up and down. Lou did the same to her. He was concerned that she was lightly dressed for the time of year. She had a small backpack but no visible food or portable shelter. Just the emergency sleeping bag. Her long black hair was tied with a beaded hair tie, the kind often used by native women. She had brown skin and was clearly in very good shape. But she was holding her ankle, and Lou assumed she was injured. After an awkward moment, she said, "I hurt my ankle."

Lou took that as permission to kneel next to her. "May I?" He took the petite ankle into the palm of his large hand. He had a doctor's demeanor, even though he was just a certified EMT, something he had renewed the previous year because no one in their little community of cabins had medical training. "It looks swollen," he said, "but not too bad." Her feet were well calloused, and it was clear she was an experienced runner who had also run barefoot. Her legs, and particularly her calves, were scratched and bruised.

When Lou touched her, he sensed her guard coming down. He had been assigned to cases on the Indian Reservation just before retirement because Native Americans respected their elders, and his gray hair was an asset in the investigations. She smiled but did not offer any words. "I've got a couple energy bars." He reached into his pack and pulled out the calorie dense treats. Without hesitation, she accepted. Then he handed her a small bottle of sports drink. He had two more energy bars and another bottle of sports drink that he placed near her pack.

"I won't be needing these, and you will," he said quietly.

The October sun was at a low angle. It struggled to penetrate the dense willows. A light breeze danced across the tops of the browning leaves, but the inner circle was protected. It was a perfect natural shelter. Lou sat down in the grass across from the runner and took some athletic tape from his medical kit. "I can tape it for you if you would like," he said in a soft voice.

Her face said, "Yes," but there were no words. He wrapped the tape around her calf until he had an anchor then reached the tape around the ankle, building additional support for the moderate injury. "I'm guessing it's not going to do much good to tell you to stay off this for a couple days," Lou said in a scolding tone. The young woman smiled.

"So, this will give you the support you need to keep moving."

There was a pause, and she said, "Thank you."

Up until this point Lou had avoided direct eye contact with her. He knew humans were sometimes like wild animals. Direct eye contact from strangers could be threatening. But she had accepted his food, drink, and medical care. Perhaps now she would answer his question. He looked directly into her soft brown eyes. Even though he had only known her for five minutes, she had a daughter-like demeanor. His long experience in quickly sizing up people told him she was a good person. The kind of person he had spent his whole life trying to protect.

"So, what are you running from, young lady?" he said in a calming voice. He had interrogated hundreds of suspects, but this was not an interrogation. He was truly concerned. But he didn't expect her to talk without much coaxing. He was wrong. She took the fly on the first cast, and two hours later, she was still talking when they both detected a shift in the background noise of the forest. Lou put his finger up to his lips to signal quiet.

The insects, the birds, and the other critters had all gone silent. Lou slowly rolled over and lay flat on his belly, looking around the bases of the willows. A few hundred feet out into the meadow, he could see movement. He held still. Very still. Feet started moving closer, then he could see the legs and the full figure. It was a man with dark sunglasses, black pants, and a black shirt standing with his back to their hiding place. He was scanning the trees and looking for clues.

Lou looked at Kwayah, but she was already in motion, getting ready to run. He handed her his medical kit, all his remaining food, and the sports drink. She smiled and placed it in her pack. Then he quietly took his windbreaker out of his pack along with his handgun. Kwayah was surprised to see the weapon. And even more surprised to see what was on the back of his windbreaker. Lou put the weapon in his pocket so it could be easily accessed.

Then he stood, careful not to put his head up all the way and reveal his position. As he did, he whispered to his new friend, "Go. And be safe."

She nodded, and Lou started towards the man in black. After the first step, he felt a hand on his arm. He turned back, and the young woman who he had only known for two hours buried her head in his chest.

"Thank you," she said. "We will meet again."

He nodded and exited the safety of the willows for the meadow.

# CHAPTER 14

Lou picked up his fishing rod so he would "fit in," and moved obviously so as not to seem suspicious to the man in black. As he emerged from the willows, he noticed the man had been joined by two others dressed in worn camo hunting garb. When he could see that they had seen him, he placed his hand in his pocket, directly on the revolver, and walked confidently towards the trio.

It was a strange group. Two white people dressed like budget hunters, with Walmart gear. Then a Native American man dressed to intimidate in an urban environment. The Indian was ill equipped to be in this wilderness setting. He had silver-toed cowboy boots that were more for show than for go. They were already scuffed, and he was standing as if his feet were blistered. The two in hunting garb had rifles on their shoulders, but they were overweight and out of shape. As hunters, they would likely be the ones who never pulled the trigger unless they were a few hundred feet from a road. Hauling out their kill was beyond their capacity. One of them, who Lou had mistaken for a man, was puffing on a cigarette. As Lou approached, she tossed the cigarette butt in the grass and crushed it with her foot.

"Hunting season is over," Lou said without a formal greeting to the pair.

The man in black smiled a big, well-rehearsed, white toothy smile and said," Well, you never know what or who you'll run into out here." Then he swatted a bug away from his face and nodded to his partners who were already in a mild defensive stance. When they saw the fishing pole, the two in camo gear relaxed. Lou stopped twenty feet in front of the trio so he could see all three of them if anything changed quickly. He kept his hand on the revolver in his pocket, and he noticed with satisfaction when they noticed he had his hand on something big in his pocket.

"So, what brings you up into this quiet bit of heaven fully armed?" Lou asked. He had not used his cop voice since he retired, and he was glad to see it still worked. He then waited for the lie. He expected a lie. These were the kind of people who told you what they thought you wanted to hear. A lie is what he got.

"We're looking for a friend," the man in black who wanted to do all the talking explained. "A young woman who is missing from the reservation."

Now he was playing the Indian card, Lou noted. So many white people didn't understand the relationship between Indian Reservations and the rest of the country. Often Indians would take advantage of that to bend the rules or even break the law. This man made it sound like the woman belonged to the Indian Reservation and needed to be returned.

"Which reservation?" Lou asked directly.

"Shoshone," the smoking woman answered in a husky, tobacco-strained voice. It was the first time Lou noticed that one of the camo-clad sidekicks was a different gender.

Then the man in black said, "Fort Washakie…"

"That's several hundred miles from here," Lou said. "What has this young woman done?"

There was a pause, and the smoking woman stepped forward. Lou stiffened and gripped the revolver in his pocket. It was enough to keep the woman from moving closer.

"This woman has escaped from custody. And we're here to find her. I am Sergeant Gare, and this is Corporal Diggins." She was now using her police voice, but Lou could tell she was hiding something.

"Are you law enforcement?" he asked.

"Yes," Gare said.

"What agency?"

"Wyoming State Corrections," she said.

"So, you're prison guards and not law enforcement," Lou said.

"Not much difference," Gare said, squirming with annoyance at Lou's familiarity with the legal system.

"And who is this fellow?" Lou asked Gare about the man in black. Again, the toothy smile as the man stepped forward to shake Lou's hand. But Lou stiffened and took two steps backwards, still holding the revolver in his windbreaker pocket.

"I'm Randy Wild Horse, from the reservation," he said, still in a friendly tone. He pretended that the failed handshake had not happened.

"So, let me get this straight," Lou said. "You two prison guards lost one of your prisoners in the next state over. You hooked up with this reservation civilian and came up into the mountains of Utah to look for her. And you think she's running up this meadow towards the High Uintahs Wilderness?"

Gare did not move. She didn't say anything. The man in black dropped his toothy grin. Behind his dark glasses, he stared at the tall, white man obstructing their path. While they were apparently considering the price of doing something violent, Lou took the initiative. He surprised himself and pointed his pocket at them, leaving what was in it to their imaginations.

"I would appreciate it if you two hunters would place those cannons on the ground. I don't feel comfortable with your hands near a trigger." His voice was firm. His stance was unwavering. He could see in their eyes that all three of them assumed he had a handgun in the pocket of his dark blue windbreaker, but none of them had the courage to find out for sure.

"You first." He locked eyes on Gare but carefully watched the others in his peripheral vision. The woman begrudgingly placed her rifle on the ground in slow motion while keeping direct eye contact with Lou. Next, Lou motioned to the other prison guard. After a pause and a glaring look, he placed his hunting rifle on the ground in a motion that communicated resentment. "Now you!" He turned slightly to the man in black. "Empty your pockets, and take that knife out of your boot." Running Bear registered surprised that his concealment was visible from twenty feet away.

"I would like to invite you all to take ten steps backwards. Don't turn around, just walk backwards," Lou said. He was relieved that this disarming process had gone off without a hitch. The trio complied and moved slowly away from the weapons.

Gare erupted, "You are impeding a law enforcement activity, and that's going to get you in big trouble, mister."

"I know law enforcement, and you are not law enforcement," Lou told the woman. Then he bent over and picked up the first rifle. He opened the chamber and removed all the bullets. Then he took out the firing pin and removed the bolt action. He threw them both out into the thick grass in the meadow then threw the rifle the other direction.

"You are just a couple of minimum wage prison guards who are working with this bad ass meth head with false teeth to find a woman who is trying to get out of your little corrupt kingdom."

Then he took the second rifle and dismantled it in the same way and threw the pieces in different places around the meadow. He picked up the knife, inspected it, and put it in his pocket.

"I'm going to keep this," he said. "You need to know that you will not find her in this meadow, or on that mountain, or along the highway, or anyplace. If you do, by some miracle, find her in Utah, where you have no authority or jurisdiction, and you take her back to Wyoming, then you have committed a federal crime, and that's when all my buddies from the FBI come in and charge you with kidnapping."

Lou then looked at the man in black. "You, pretty boy, would not last twenty minutes in a federal prison. And you two 'law enforcement professionals,'" he said sarcastically, "would be welcomed with opened arms by the inmates then turned into pin cushions or punching bags."

Lou looked at his watch then said, "You will not leave this meadow for the next hour. If you wish, you may spend that time looking for the pieces of your weapons that I 'accidentally' dropped in the grass when I was helping you get them unjammed. After an hour, you can return to that silly looking black Jeep parked down at the trailhead. Then I suggest you get in your vehicles, ask Mr. Google maps which is the fastest way back to Wyoming, then do exactly what he says, or she says, depending on your setting.

"I think I'm going to go back to not catching any fish in this low-water river." Lou turned the volume up on his voice as he turned and walked towards the willows where he had left Kwayah. As he did, the trio could see for the first time the large, yellow letters on the back of his windbreaker that spelled out "FBI."

# CHAPTER 15

Not long after midnight, Nate, Caleb, and Boo pulled into the Uintah County Correctional Facility to spend the night in jail. At least that's what they were joking about when Nate buzzed through the security gate. Uintah County was too cheap to put them up in a motel. Instead, the county jail facility had an overnight room where officers could get some sleep if the weather made roads or the freeway impassable. Snow and wind closed I-80 two or three times every winter. When that happened, hotels would instantly up their rates and still fill up with stranded truckers and cross-country drivers. Sheriff Rondo Clark had taken an unused room in the staff building next to the jail and turned it into a guest room for law enforcement who couldn't get home in a blizzard. But even more often, the guestroom was offered to traveling families who had unexpectedly broken down and couldn't afford a hotel. On many occasions, the room had included free or discounted car repairs, food money collected from police dispatchers and deputies, and winter clothing from the local thrift store.

The cots in the room were the same as the ones used in the jail, but the mattresses, sheets, and bed covers were a significant upgrade to what the prisoners got in the neighboring building. Nate had told Caleb what to expect. He had stayed there before during the blizzard of 2009. Before jail, the two had stopped at Paff's and picked up some fine Mexican food rather than risk eating prison food. Either way, Boo got his favorite fixings from a can. Nate always carried a few meals of dog food in his pickup truck with his go bag. He never knew when he might be doing an overnight with his dog.

In the end, the quality of the accommodations didn't matter. After Caleb filled up on a green chili burrito that he ate while Nate was driving because he couldn't wait, he wanted to collapse on the first flat surface he saw. As soon as he entered the sparsely-furnished guest room at the jail, he plopped face down on the closest bunk. With great efficiency of movement, he reached down and took off his shoes then went face down again and only moved twice in the next ten hours.

Boo was also tired. But he preferred the cool, firm surface of the floor to the bouncy springs of human beds. Nate put the dog's water dish down in a corner and broke open the can of dog food. Boo laid down in a position where he could see the room then curled up head on tail and slept.

Nate took his time. He took a shower and changed into clean gym shorts and a T-shirt that was his sleepwear. Then he called Marie.

"I'm in jail," he said in a monotone voice in an attempt to tease.

"I can't afford to bail you out," she said, following the joke. "I spent all our money at Costco. Besides, I'm not sure I would want to."

Nate filled her in on the details of the search, and Marie quickly turned the conversations towards Caleb. "Are you sure it's okay to have Caleb with you? He must be bored out of his mind?" Marie had been looking forward to having Caleb as a guest in her home.

"No. He's having the time of his life." Nate looked over at the sleeping teenager. "He gets to hang out in the woods with his best friend."

"You?" said Marie.

"No," answered Nate. "Boo."

With that, Marie launched a question that went right to the core of the matter. "Why is this young woman making such an effort to get away from the prison when she only has a short time left on her sentence?"

"We don't know," said Nate. "When Boo catches up with her, I hope she'll tell us."

"At the rate she's moving, Nate, I don't think you're going to catch her." Nate always appreciated Marie's honesty, even if it sometimes hurt. He had to admit the runner had surprised him at every turn, frustrating him with nonthreatening evasion. Of course, Boo was different. It was a game for him, and he loved the pursuit.

Nate changed the subject and asked about her day, pretending to be interested when Marie talked about the gossip of their small town. When the end-of-day words of a good marriage were spoken, Nate said, "Good night. I love you, honey," and placed the cell phone on a charger. Within a few minutes, he too was asleep on the cot.

Before the sun penetrated the curtainless windows in the sparse room, Nate was up and getting ready to go. He let Caleb and Boo sleep while he tiptoed out of the room and drove a few blocks from the jail to a café to meet Daisey Mae.

"I'm sorry I had to abandon the search. My boss expected me to go back and run the prison," Daisey Mae said with a smirk. "When I got back from our day together, about half the night shift was either taking personal days off or calling in sick. Something is going on with that bunch."

"Yeah," said Nate. "I think some of them are out looking for your prisoner. Yesterday, I met this super greasy guy from the Shoshone reservation with a couple of yahoos who I recognized as two of your night guards. They were following us around by Sulphur Creek."

"Did you get a plate?" Daisey Mae asked.

"No. I was busy trying to head her off at the reservoir. Rondo had the west end sealed off, and we had her trapped."

"I heard what happened there. Did she really swim across the reservoir?" asked the warden.

"She did," said Nate. "She's amazing. Quite the athlete."

Nate paused and stirred his coffee. He didn't like leaving a search like this unfinished. But he was also feeling the need to get back to Lincoln and his duties as a deputy and a husband. "I'm not sure how much more time I can give you on this search, particularly now that she has likely crossed over into Utah," he said.

"Don't worry," said Daisey Mae. "Rondo and I called your sheriff yesterday and reported in for you. He said we could have you for another week if necessary. I hope that's okay?"

"Thanks," said Nate, not really meaning it.

"I also called Summit County in Utah because I think that's where she's headed."

"Good," said Nate, stirring his coffee again, collecting his thoughts for the difficult idea that was coming next.

"Warden, I don't think we're seeing the whole picture here. I have never seen such a committed fugitive, and I want to know what she's running from, who she's running to, and why."

"So do I," said Daisey Mae. "So do I."

# CHAPTER 16

"So, this is what it's like to be a zombie," Caleb said to himself. He had a vague recollection of waking to the sterile public restroom used by jail staff in his dirty jeans, T-shirt, and muddy shoes. Then he stutter stepped through the hall and into the parking lot, collapsing and falling asleep on the back seat of the pickup. Boo relinquished his usual spot on the bench and lay dejected on the floor where he couldn't see the passing country. At some point, Caleb remembered stopping for a drive-thru breakfast on the way out of Evanston. Nate passed the food back to Caleb who suspended his exhaustion and devoured the bland fast-food breakfast sandwich as if he had not eaten in five days. Then he returned to dreamland while Nate drove the twenty-seven miles into Utah towards the starting point for the search.

With a dog and a teenage boy in a catatonic state, Nate turned off the scenic highway and onto a dirt road then bounced his pickup toward the trailhead for the East Fork of the Bear River. As he pulled into the parking lot, he was surprised to see the ratty pickup truck and new model black Jeep Rubicon at the far end. He was even more surprised to see the pickup truck was listing to one side with flat tires on the driver's side. A tall, athletic older man wearing an FBI windbreaker was standing between the two vehicles. He was starting to let the air out of the tires on the jeep. He looked up, showing surprise at seeing Nate's law enforcement vehicle from Wyoming in that remote part of Utah. Nate was equally surprised to see someone he admired and respected doing a teenage prank on the only two cars in the trailhead parking lot.

Nate stepped out of the cab and walked towards the man. He left Caleb to take his time to wake up. But Boo was already to go. His tail began to wag, and he tapped his nose on the window, asking to be let out. The men shook hands then embraced in a sincere brotherly hug. That kind of affection from Nate was only reserved for very good friends. Then he turned to wave the recently awakened Caleb over. Caleb stepped out of the truck, and as he did, Boo bounded over to him then ran towards the stranger, his tail sailing in the air. He had the "play with me" prance going full-bore that came as a bonus feature with golden retrievers. The stranger saw the dog coming and extended another brotherly embrace. They were clearly friends. The man picked up a stick from the ground, flashed it at Boo, then launched it across the parking lot. Before he had completed the throw, Boo was prancing towards the expected landing point to do what every piece of DNA in his body told him to do, retrieve. He picked up the stick and returned to the stranger for an encore.

"Caleb," Nate said with pride, "this is my good friend Lou Bertram. Lou was the FBI agent who helped crack a human trafficking group that was using truckers to move people around Wyoming. Then he gave Lincoln County all the credit in the media." Nate had told Caleb the story before. It was Nate's biggest success as a one-size-fits-all law enforcement agent in his small community. One day he was working with the FBI to bust a national crime ring; the next day he was giving out parking tickets at the county fair.

"Let's give credit where credit is due," Lou said, as he pulled the stick from Boo's mouth and launched it again across the parking lot. "We would never have found where they were hiding those people were it not for this genius dog."

In a playful tone, Nate asked, "So what's a retired FBI agent doing committing an act of petty vandalism on a pair of out-of-state vehicles?"

"Help me deflate the tires on this second vehicle then give me a ride back to my cabin," Lou said. "I'll tell you why I'm doing this."

"Hope the Summit County Sheriff doesn't come along and arrest us," Nate said.

"They don't even know this part of the county exists," Lou said. "We pay our taxes, and they stay away."

Nate notice Caleb's grin as the two grown men bantered back and forth. He caught the irony as the two men, with clothing identifying them as law enforcement, bent over and deflated the tires on the black Jeep like reckless teenagers in prank mode. Then they piled into the cab. As they drove on a maze of dirt roads and passed through two locked gates, Lou told the story of finding the runner and the stand-off that had occurred with the prison guards and Indian gangster earlier that morning in the meadow.

"I think I was able to get her a pretty good head start," Lou bragged. "I intimidated them into dismantling their weapons and waiting in the meadow for an hour. They're probably still looking for gun parts, and when they finally get to the parking lot, they'll be cursing and calling for roadside service. At least we slowed them down."

"Why didn't you hold them for the sheriff?" Caleb asked.

"Because I couldn't identify anything they were doing that was illegal," the former FBI agent explained. "Besides, if I did, I'd have to tell them about that young Indian woman."

"But that's who we're looking for," Caleb said.

The conversation grew serious as Nate explained how they were on the third day of tracking the woman, how Daisey Mae had started with them, and how the runner had escaped at every turn. Nate also mentioned how the slick native man from the Indian reservation in Fort Washakie had joined the search, along with the two others he suspected of being prison guards.

The cabin was a simple "off the grid" building at the center of an aspen grove. At this altitude, the aspens had long since turned yellow, then brown, and were now dropping their leaves. Caleb noticed a full deck of solar panels and a satellite dish. He also could smell bacon cooking from outside in the driveway.

"Smells like we have breakfast coming," Lou said. "I promise it's going to be a lot better than this crap." He held up the bag containing Nate's fast-food breakfast that he had not yet eaten."

The smells that were triggering human hunger were driving the dog to uncontainable anticipation. "Bacon teaches us how a dog feels when he is hungry," Nate said. "They can smell what's coming before they see it."

As the two men and the boy who was almost a man entered the cabin, Lou's wife was putting the finishing touches on a breakfast spread that was a teenager's dream. Hot biscuits just out of the warming oven on the old wood burning stove. Wild berry jam from mason jars canned last fall. Scrambled eggs fresh from the chicken coop behind the cabin. Fresh fruit from the Walmart in Evanston. Hash browns. Gravy with chunks of spicy sausage. And bacon. A mountain of bacon.

Lou's wife greeted him with a kiss and Nate with a hug. Then she focused on Caleb.

"Who's this deputy?"

Before Caleb could offer his reason for being there, Nate jumped in. "He's a young man who helps us train Boo. He was with us when the call came in, and because this isn't a dangerous call, we decided to let him come along." Then Nate winked at Caleb, and Lou's wife offered a hug, and they all sat down to a mid-morning breakfast.

While Caleb was eating second and third helpings, Lou pulled out his laptop and typed out a message. "I just sent a message with the license plate from the Jeep Rubicon to an FBI agent I trained who's stationed at Fort Washakie. We'll see what he says."

"I thought this would be over in a day," Nate said. "I thought Boo would track her, she would be out of shape, and she would be ready to come home. Nothing has gone as expected."

"It never does," said Lou, putting the credibility of his years of service in the FBI behind his voice. "I don't think you're going to catch her," he said. "She's in her element now and moving too fast."

"If we don't, those three others might catch her first," said Nate.

"Or the weather." Lou added. "It's about ready to turn winter here, and up at higher elevations, they've already had one snowstorm."

"We have to get out in front of her," Nate said.

"Why don't you get the Summit County Sheriff involved?" Lou's wife asked.

"We really need more manpower," said Nate. "But this is a minimum-security prisoner from Wyoming and just not a priority for Utah law enforcement. They told us as much when we asked for permission to search in their jurisdiction."

"I'm willing to help," Lou said. "But I can't keep up with either of you in the woods, so I'll need to stay near my car."

"Well, for starters, you can tell us what you know about her. We need to understand her mindset," Nate said.

Lou was not reluctant about recounting the details of the story he had heard in the willow hideaway that morning. "She is running for her own safety," he said. "She thinks the prison guards are going to come after her because she knows too much and is trusted by Daisey Mae. She's also running because her grandmother may only have a few days to live. She is very close to her grandmother and has trusted her to care for her little daughter while she serves out her term."

"What's the story on her conviction?" Nate asked.

"The bozo in black in the Jeep who has been chasing her around, he was her husband's drug supplier. Once the husband was gone, the dealer dude wanted her to pay the money her husband owed. Well, she had never seen any money. He brought a charge of assault, and with the help of a corrupt cop and public defender, they got her a two-year sentence."

"We can't just let her run," Nate said. "Sooner or later things will go bad for her."

"That's true," said Lou. "But I don't think she would trust us to help, and I'm sure she would not trust prison system."

"I spoke with the warden."

"Daisey Mae?" Lou interrupted.

"Yes. She has a pretty good grasp on this situation and wants the best for her. Between the three of us, we ought to be able to figure this out."

"First, we have to catch her."

Caleb laughed when they got out a paper map. He was used to Nate doing things low tech. Nate drew a line from the Mormon camp to the reservoir and to the East Fork Meadow. "If we move, we could see her passing across the big open space at Christmas Meadows," Lou said. "Maybe I can talk her into trusting us to make things right."

"If we don't catch her, she'll be in the high country with a storm just a day away," Nate said.

"Let's give it a try," said Lou. Then he smiled at Caleb and handed him a plate with the last of the bacon.

# CHAPTER 17

Caleb sat on the back of the pickup truck in full view of the three-mile-long Christmas Meadows in the Wasatch-Cache National Forest. Boo sat next to him, nose in the wind, trying to inventory every smell in the valley. The binoculars and a handheld radio were within quick reach. The truck was parked on the north side of the meadow on a high point where Caleb could see the Stillwater Fork of the Bear River meandering through willow, meadow grass, and over an occasional beaver dam. This was a well-known spot for landscape photographers who put the river and the meadow in the foreground leading to the majestic Ostler's Peak in the background. This spot had produced more than one award-winning travel calendar photograph.

But Caleb was not to be distracted by the natural beauty of the High Uintahs. His job was to watch Boo. If Boo's nose moved, if he saw a twitch or interest, then he would grab the binoculars and check it out. If he saw the runner, he was to call on the radio. So far, all he had seen were deer and a moose.

If Caleb saw her, Nate and Lou were supposed to intercept her on the other side of the meadow. Nate was halfway up a tree in the upper meadow, scanning the space from a different angle. Lou was on the deck of one of the Forest Service lease cabins in the lower meadow. The cabin community was closed for the season, but the roads were not. Lou had a mobility advantage. A road stretched a mile on the far side of the lower meadow and served as cabin access. Lou had picked up an e-bike at his cabin and could shoot quietly along the road and quickly intercept the runner if she passed in the lower meadow. They assumed the runner would not pass in the middle point because she would see the pickup truck at the high point overlooking the widest, most exposed part of the meadow.

So, the plan was good. The trap was set. The team was ready. Nate and Lou assumed all they needed to do was get within earshot of the runner and promise to protect her from the posse of night guards who were closing in. "If we can get her to talk, we can get her to stay," Nate had said. Nothing was further from the truth.

Every twenty minutes on the second, Lou came on the radio and checked in with Nate and Caleb. Because Nate only had one police handheld radio, and because Lou and Caleb were not authorized to be on police frequencies, they used store-bought family band radios that worked line of sight.

Even so, Caleb felt pretty important with a radio and an important assignment.

When he returned to Iowa and reported his fall break adventure to his friends, they wouldn't believe him. He was doing real police work pursuing a fugitive while they did hard manual labor helping with the harvest.

In the first twenty-minute period, Caleb diligently scanned the meadow, following every movement. In the second twenty-minute period, Boo started to lose interest. His nose had told him the news of Christmas Meadows. Caleb took him around the truck a few times to keep him from dozing off. After two hours, the runner was clearly overdue, and both Caleb and Boo were doing everything they could to stay awake and alert. They were sitting fully exposed in the sun, and even though it had been below freezing overnight, they were pretty hot sitting on the tailgate.

After checking in with the team, Caleb returned to his tailgate perch. Nothing in the meadow. Nothing in the trees along the meadow. The still waters in the pooling river reflected the brown grass and the green spruce trees. It was a motionless scene. Then Boo slowly jumped from the bed of the truck and wandered over to a piece of grass to do his business. He went fifty feet further to a small stream for a drink of water. Then he turned his back towards the truck in a slow-motion version of a head snap, which was a prerequisite to a find. He meandered back to the truck and settled in the shade on the passenger side of the vehicle. Meanwhile, Caleb kept his eyes on the meadow, thinking the dog would soon join him when he tired of being alone in the shade.

About that time, Caleb had the distinct feeling he was being watched. He had experienced that same feeling before and had learned to trust his instincts. Two years before when he was lost in the Wyoming wilderness, before Boo and Nate rescued him, he also had felt like he was being watched. Later, he saw a large bull moose tracking him from afar. This time, he felt like they were human eyes not animal eyes. In a rare deep conversation, Caleb had once explained this feeling to his father. To his surprise, the distant, excessively rational professor-want-to-be said, "I believe you. Our eyes and our other senses pick up a lot more information than we can process in the short-term memory part of our brains. Intuition is when you have lots of information generated by an active environment, but your brain is sending that information to the long-term memory part of your brain. You're just reacting to what you saw when you were really looking for something else."

Caleb liked that his father understood and agreed with him, even if he didn't always follow his father's academic explanations. But in the current moment, Caleb was trying to process the feeling, scanning the meadow and the trees, looking for anyone who was looking at him.

Finally, he picked up the radio and called. "Nate?"

"Yes? Everything okay?"

"Yes. Just doing a radio check."

"All good here. Lou?"

"Got my eyes on the moose, so she's not nearby because the moose would have her ears up."

"Okay," said Caleb.

He put down the radio and looked over the silent, still meadow. Then it occurred to him he hadn't seen Boo for a few minutes. The dog was not in the truck's bed, and he was not on the sunny side of the truck.

So, he scooted across the tailgate then casually stepped to the shady side of the truck. His dog lay in the cool gravel, tail wagging, enjoying the affection of a small woman with waist-length dark hair and cool brown eyes.

Caleb wasn't scared. He wasn't even surprised. For an awkward moment, he watched the woman scratch the dog's ears. Then he said, "Kwayah?"

"Yes," she said with a quiet smile.

"How long have you been there?"

"More than an hour." There was a long pause as Caleb digested what he had just heard. Then he asked, "Why are you hiding here? Next to the truck?" He thought she might want to surrender, something Nate had been predicting since day one.

"Because the easiest place to go unnoticed is in plain sight. I was in the clump of trees when you pulled up in the truck. I thought you had seen me, but you were all focused on the meadow and not the trees."

"Wow," said Caleb. "So, you probably heard our entire plan?"

"Yes," she said, laughing. "You are the young man they call Caleb." He nodded. "The friend to this fine animal?" Boo looked up. He seemed to know they were talking about him, but he didn't want her to stop scratching his ears. Caleb nodded again. "The young man who as a boy survived in the wilderness for three nights?"

Caleb was always surprised what he was remembered for. "Yes," he said, in a quiet voice as if speaking loudly would scare her into running again.

"Now, I'm part of the team, with Nate and Lou. We're trying to…"

"Hunt me. Capture me. Take me back to prison," she finished his sentence.

"Well, yeah. That's how it started," Caleb said. "Now we just want to protect you from that sleaze bag guy in the Jeep and the night guards' posse that seems to want to hurt you."

"So, you're still going to hunt me, capture me, and take me back to prison?"

"No, I think you've got it wrong," said Caleb. "That warden with the funny name…"

"Daisey Mae," the runner filled in the blank.

"She wants to protect you."

"I'm not sure she can."

"Nate can. He's a deputy sheriff in Wyoming. And Lou. You met Lou this morning. He used to work for the FBI. He's the guy who stopped the bad guys from getting you this morning." Caleb's voice was getting more excited as he tried to convince the woman they had been chasing for three days now to give up.

Before Caleb could say more, the radio crackled. It was Nate.

"Hey, Caleb, you okay? I can't see you on the back of the truck," he said.

Caleb picked up the radio and said, "I'm okay." Then he looked at the woman. She was small and unthreatening, yet her legs and arm were muscular. She could surely outrun him and probably out fight him. He didn't want to find out.

"He'll be checking on you again in twenty minutes," she said. "Better sit on the tailgate and face the meadow." Caleb complied. He knew the longer he could keep her there the better the chance was she would stay.

"What are you going to do?" he asked.

"For now," she said, "I'm going to scratch his ears."

# CHAPTER 18

Caleb sat on the tailgate, facing the meadow. He waited for her to speak, but finally when she didn't, he asked, "Why did you run?"

The silence continued, but he could hear her shifting positions, getting ready to speak. "I mean you just had a short time left on your sentence. In a few weeks, you'd be released, and you could go back to your life. Why did you mess it all up?"

"Look at the river," she said. Caleb looked at the appropriately named Stillwater Fork snake through the brown matted grass. He wondered what she wanted him to see.

"You can see where the river runs over the rocks. Where there is motion, the water is clear."

"Yes."

"But where the water is still, it is clouded with silt."

"Oh, yes." Caleb could see how the river seemed to break free of the meadow in places and become a river again. A moving, dynamic body.

"My river was clouded. I was in a place I did not belong. I am losing my Wici-ci. My Grandmother. She is my daughter's protector and caregiver. Without her, strangers will take over and raise my little one. In prison, the water was not clear. I could not see who I could trust. I needed to break free so I could see. So I could be safe. Now I am clear. My daughter needs a mother. My grandmother needs a granddaughter. I may need to cut my hair."

The last three things she said caught Caleb off guard. He was surprised that this young woman, who was just ten years older than he was, had a daughter who was born before she started serving time in prison. He also was struck by the idea that a grandmother would *need* a granddaughter. His grandmother spent time in her garden and going on cruises. Sometimes she needed help to move things that were heavy or getting picked up at the airport. But she didn't need Caleb. And finally, that thing about cutting hair. Her hair was long and beautiful. Why did she need to escape prison to cut her hair?

As Caleb was processing these questions, and thinking how he might respond, Kwayah spoke again in a slow, methodical rhythm. "Your story and my story are not different," she said. "I know your story is one of going from cloudy to clear because I read about how you ran away from the picnic in Lincoln. You ran away from what your mother wanted. You ran away from your aunt and your bully cousin. You had done nothing wrong. You were not safe, and you felt you would be safer going home. I am not much different than you."

Caleb was surprised she remembered the details of his survival story even though it was old news to most people.

She continued, "I grew up in a town called White Rock on the Ute Indian Reservation on the other side of these mountains. I had many cousins and good friends. Kind people in a beautiful place, but it was also full of danger. My ancestors worried that the bear would come out of the mountains and eat their children. They worried that the spring waters running high would wash the children away. And sometimes they did.

"The bear comes no more. And bridges cross over the waters. But new dangers exist that take many children and even their parents. My parents were taken by alcohol. First my father then my mother. The crazy water that he drank caused him to crash his car. The same poison sent my mother to a hospital for rehabilitation. When she got out, she was ashamed and has never returned home. My grandmother said she became a tumbleweed with a broken spirit."

The story captured Caleb's full attention. So much so that he found himself sitting next to her on the shady side of the truck. Both had their hands on the dog. When she paused, he waited then, with reverence, said, "Please continue."

"My grandmother raised me. She is the mother to my mother, and we were both broken-hearted about the fast death of my father and the slow death of my mother because of the poison drink that our ancestors did not know.

"Every day, I would ride the school bus to Fort Duchesne and learn the language and stories of the white people. When I would come home, before I could play with my friends, Grandmother taught me in the language and stories of our people. She taught me to listen before I speak, to watch the sky and understand the weather, to keep my body clean and my mind free."

"When did you learn to run?" Caleb asked.

"Running came naturally for me. In White Rock, people noticed I could run faster than other girls and boys my age. So, my cousins and other people would ask me to deliver fresh bread or meat to those people who did not live in town. As I got older, I was asked by the principal to run on the track team at my school. A few could run short distances faster than I could, but no one, not even the boys, could run farther than I could. I won every distance race."

"Wow," said Caleb. "I've never won a single race. I'm not fast."

"But you have other gifts," the runner said with confidence. "Running is my gift."

Caleb enjoyed hearing what she said and looked up, urging her to continue with his eyes.

"In high school, running was my ticket to see beyond White Rock and the community of our reservation. As soon as I was old enough, the athletic director in the school entered me in everything. I ran in community races. I ran in track meets against white people from city schools. And I ran against other reservation schools. The athletic director appointed himself to be our track coach then he recruited a couple of my friends to be on the track team and travel with us, even though they were not very interested in running."

She paused and scanned the meadow then said under her breath, "I think the window is closing." Then she continued with her story.

"In high school, my training program was to run home from school. It was ten or fifteen miles, depending on which route I would take. Sometimes, I would run the trails or along the road. My people got used to seeing me pounding away at the pavement, and they would often wave with pride at the girl who was setting the running records for the high school and later for all high schools."

"So, you won all the time at the track meets?"

"Yes. I always won, and I always came home with a medal or a trophy. They filled my bedroom, and I wanted my grandmother to make room for them in the living room, but she would not. Sometimes sports reporters would call and want to talk to me on the phone, but she would not let them through. She would tell me that a newspaper article, trophy or a medal, or a broken record did not tell me who I was. 'Be who you are not who they want you to be,' she would say. 'Remember your people.'"

I've never earned a trophy, Caleb thought. Then he wondered what it would be like to have a room full of trophies.

"The more I raced, the more fame I gathered. People knew me. People talked about me. I was famous, and I was proud. But my grandmother feared for me because she could see my world was becoming cloudy like the dark waters in the river. Unclear. I think she was afraid of losing another daughter, so she gave me more rules and required me to be home by a certain time. These were things I did not like. We also no longer talked about the ways of our people. I was too busy. Still, she would speak Ute to me, but I would speak back in English.

When I was a senior in high school, two things happened that tore me from my roots. First, some of the best colleges in America invited me to come and run on their track teams. They were part of my country but far away from my people. They invited me to fly on airplanes and visit their campuses. They introduced me to black people, other brown people, and a few Indians from other tribes. They were all segregated in diversity clubs, as if skin color was what defined us. I was worried that I could not keep up in the classroom. But I was always introduced to a tutor with dark skin who said they had never met a real *Indian.*

"I did not know where I wanted to go to school, but I was beginning to see a life for me beyond the reservation and away from my people. I also made connections with people from the different organizations that support track and field competitions in college, including several members of the US Olympic Committee. To me, the Olympics were a television event, but for the first time in my life, I could see myself running in the Olympics.

"The second thing that happened to me was George Thunder Cloud. George was a lousy runner, but he was a handsome young boy from the Shoshone Reservation in Wyoming. I met him when I was a junior at an All-Indian track meet, and he was very nice to me. I had never had a boyfriend, and so it felt very good to have a boy interested in me.

"We texted every day, and we would see each other at track meets sometimes. I got grounded once became they caught us kissing under the bleachers, and I almost missed my event. But that did not slow us down.

"Towards the middle of my senior year, sometime in the winter, George and I arranged to meet in southern Wyoming and go on a real date. We planned it for weeks. I told my grandmother I was going to an indoor track meet then I borrowed my friend's car and drove over the east end of the Uintahs to Rock Springs, Wyoming. We met at the high school track where we had run. He took me to a restaurant, and we went miniature golfing. Then we went somewhere outside of town and camped together under a mountain of blankets in the back of his old pickup. We stayed together for the next two days, happy and carefree, and I thought I was in love. But after the second night, my grandmother, who had never before sent a text message, asked me to come home. She was worried, so I returned.

"I think my grandmother knew where I had been. But I returned and went on with my life as if nothing had changed. I trained every day. I did my school work. I competed. I won. But I also stopped hearing from George. Oh, he would answer my texts, but it was clear he was not as interested as he had once been."

Caleb was shocked. She was much older but very pretty and very nice. He was just at the age where he was interested in girls and could not imagine neglecting someone like her. Even so, he acknowledged that girls were a complete mystery.

"So, what happened next?" he asked.

"I needed to sign a letter of intent in order to declare which scholarship I would take. I chose UCLA in Los Angeles, not because I liked the school or the coach or anything else other than they were close to the beach. Before visiting their campus, I had never been to a beach. So, I picked them because I could run on the beach every day and learn to surf. I was already a pretty good swimmer, and I liked the idea of swimming in the ocean.

"But my dreams of an oceanfront education came crashing down. In April, I went into the clinic to do a full checkup to make sure I did not have any medical problems. UCLA required the checkup before they finalized the scholarship. The doctor asked to meet with my grandmother and me and share the results of the tests. I could tell the doctor was worried, and I asked if there was anything wrong.

"'There is nothing wrong,' she said with a frown.

"'Then I will be able to run for the Bruins next year,' I said, seeking reassurance.

"'I don't think so,' she said. 'You are pregnant.'"

# CHAPTER 19

"It was like a silent bomb going off. I watched the destruction of my future in those three words. My grandmother put her arms around me and held me. At some point, we talked, and eventually she helped me see a future with my child. But that took some time, and it did not happen before the elder network went to work."

"The elder network?" Caleb asked.

"My people honor the elders among us. My grandmother, who is an elder, called another elder in Fort Washakie. That elder contacted George's parents who contacted George. It took about a month, but George and his grandmother showed up at my doorstep. He was dressed in his Sunday clothes. He had flowers and invited me to come and live with his family after the baby was born and get married when I was ready. It seemed like a sincere offer and a secure future for our baby."

Caleb was starting to see Kwayah in a different light. Now he understood why she had won over the prison guard, the Mormon youth leaders, and Lou. He felt like she had a special light that prison had not dimmed.

"My daughter was born in October, after the first north wind. After two weeks, George came down from Wyoming and picked us up, and we drove in his old pickup four hours north to my new home in Wyoming. Along the way, we stopped in Rock Springs at the home of a justice of the peace who married us in a civil ceremony. He said if we were married, his daughter could get benefits from the Shoshone tribe. So I said, 'Yes.' He promised we would have a big wedding on our first anniversary with all our family and cousins coming together. But that never happened.

"We moved into a tribal house in a remote corner of the reservation, out of sight from the nearest neighbor. It was not the mountain Wyoming I had imagined. Not like White Rock framed by mountains and a river. It was the sagebrush Wyoming. The windy, dusty, winter half the year Wyoming. I found myself caring for a new baby in a drafty dilapidated house in a miserable corner of the world with no neighbors. We had no money, except a food card and other government benefits that helped me get what I needed for my daughter. But even with that, I needed George to take me to the store which was many miles away, and he was not around much.

"When we arrived at the new home, no one greeted us. No one came to visit. Eventually George's parents came to meet their granddaughter, but they hardly spoke to me. His mom called me a member of a dirty tribe, and I found out the Shoshone looked down upon the Utes. My people were a small tribe, a dirty tribe, a tribe without stories. Of course, none of that was true, but that's what his family thought.

"A few weeks after I moved in, George drove home in a new pickup truck. 'Where did you get the money for this truck?' I asked. He told me he needed it for his work. I asked him what he was doing for work. What kept him away from his wife and daughter all day and many nights? He said the less I knew about his work, the better. When I told him we needed money for clothes for the baby, for a crib, and a car seat, he got angry. Very angry. That was the first time he hit me, and that was the first time I knew that once again the future I had imagined was destroyed.

"Living with George was like living in an earthquake zone. I never knew when there would be an eruption. When there was, it was time to get out of the house. Because I did not have a car, my only way to leave was on foot. I would strap my daughter to my back and go to one of my hiding places while George cooled down. Sometimes when I came home, he would be asleep, and sometimes, he would be gone. But he never gave an apology, and he rarely showed any affection for his daughter.

"One night, just after New Year's, there was a knock at the door. I answered because it was cool and the wind was blowing. I worried for anyone who was out that night. It was a Shoshone man who was standing in the blowing snow wearing no coat and only gym shoes with no socks. He looked like he was thirty or forty years old, but his body was much older. When he talked, he spoke in a nervous tone, and I could see his teeth were damaged. Rotted.

"'Is George here?' he asked with urgency. 'I gotta find George.'

"I told him George was gone and that I did not know when he would get back. I invited him in, but he just turned away and headed back to his truck.

"'Tell him Frank came by. Tell him I got the money and I need some more rocks. Now!' His voice turned angry, and he looked like a volcano getting ready to erupt. As he opened the door to his truck, he flashed a hand full of cash that was more money than I had ever seen.

"'I got the money,' he repeated. 'I got the money.'

"That was the first time I realized my husband was a drug dealer. Most reservations have a problem with crystal meth, or any other drug that is cheap and addictive. I knew we had that in White Rock and Fort Duchesne, but my grandmother, my ohma, had kept me away from those people. Now I was living with a man who was not only using, he was selling. After a brutal winter and a muddy spring, I started reaching out to my people, trying to come home."

Caleb's radio was blaring, and he picked it up, unhappy with the interruption to the story that explained so much.

"Caleb, this is Lou. I can't see you on the pickup truck tailgate again. Are you okay?"

"I'm fine," he said. "I'm fine." He looked at Kwayah and got permission from her eyes.

"She's here. She's with me. We're talking."

There was a long silence. Then Nate broke in, "Tell her to wait! Tell her we'll take care of her. Tell her…" The runner reached up and turned off the radio. Then she began loading her pack and preparing to leave. As she did, Caleb handed her his snack food stash from his pack.

"I guess I can't talk you into staying?"

"No," she said.

"Please finish the story," he said, half hoping to slow her down but really wanting to know what had happened next.

"In May that year, George went missing. The police came and investigated, but it seemed like a half-hearted effort. They either really did not want to find George, or they did not care that he might be dead. Later, the tribal elders visited our home and scolded me for living in poverty and not keeping the baby clean. It was their home! Then they threatened to take away my food card and other benefits. They said they needed the house for a real family. I was living scared when Randy Wild Horse came by. I think you have met Randy because he's the guy in the black Jeep who's following us around."

"What did Randy want?" Caleb asked.

"He wanted the money George owed him. I don't know if George really owed him money or if he was squeezing me for anything he could get, but after one of his threatening visits, I went Mama Bear on him. I told him I never wanted him within a mile of my daughter or me again. He was never, never welcomed at our home."

"What did he do?"

"He laughed. He said the tribal police were in his pocket. He threatened to have his way with me. He said all kinds of dirty things. So, I hit him. Right in the face. Right between the eyes. He got a nasty broken nose, and I got a broken hand. While he was walking around my living room bleeding on the floors, looking for a rag or something to put on his face, I took my daughter, put her on my back, and headed out the back door and over the hill to one of my safe hiding places. The next day when I was home again, while my daughter was napping, the tribal police came and arrested me and charged me with assault. They collected blood samples from the living room and found an unregistered handgun in the bedroom. A gun I had never seen."

"So that's how you ended up in prison?"

"Yes. I believe my lawyer took a bribe from Randy. I had no money, and he convinced me to plead guilty and serve my time because a *meth user* like me would not get an innocent verdict."

"Meth user?" Caleb stumbled.

"They found meth all around the house. Randy had planted it there, in places where the baby could get it."

"Why did they do that?" asked Caleb. The runner stood up and looked up meadow to where she could see Nate making his way across the river and towards the truck. Then she looked down meadow and spotted Lou pedaling his e-bike across the bridge. Both were about five minutes away.

"I think they wanted to use me and my daughter as leverage to get George to return the drug money he stole."

"Do you think they found him?"

"Well, yes," she said in a sad voice. "About a year ago, we got word that he died of a drug overdose in Las Vegas. But I don't believe that. It was Randy. My husband was living in a house with five other Native Americans. One of the conditions for living there was that you needed to be clean and sober. He had been off meth for some time, but some so-called-friends from the reservation in Wyoming came by to visit, and the next thing we knew, his body was found in an alley."

"I'm so sorry," Caleb said. He had such little experience with death, and he just didn't know what to say next. So, he got brave and went straight to the point. "None of this tells me why you're running from us, from Daisey Mae, from the people who want to help you."

"Because my daughter needs me. My grandmother needs me, and I might need to cut my hair," she said, repeating the strange words spoken earlier.

"What does that mean…?" Caleb pulled back his words. She was already gone. She ran a few hundred feet along the road towards Nate then turned down the road cut. Her light steps carried her over the sagebrush to the meadow grass. At the meadow grass, she sped, running with the grace of a deer. When she hit the river, the water was knee deep, but she didn't even slow down. One the far side of the meadow, she wove through the willows and up into the trees, stopping to look over the meadow and see if she was being followed.

By then Nate and Lou had joined Caleb at the pickup truck. They watched as Kwayah paused on the far side of the meadow for a moment, making brief eye contact, then disappeared into the trees.

# CHAPTER 20

"You're not going to catch her," Lou emphatically told Nate. They had been arguing about what to do next for several minutes while Nate pulled things he didn't want to carry out of his search pack and replaced them with things he would need. He scrounged up all the extra calories' worth of food, and he grabbed extra layers of clothing, winter gloves, and a wool hat. He took out his lightweight sleeping bag and put in a more heavyweight bag good to ten degrees.

Meanwhile, Lou continued to make his case. "She is too fast and too clever. She knows these mountains. Let's wait until she shows up over in Fort Duchesne at her grandmother's house or trying to see her daughter."

"If she makes it," Nate said. "She's got those bad guys from the prison and the Wyoming reservation chasing her for who knows why. And she's facing the start of winter crossing one of the toughest wilderness areas in America."

Lou continued to push back with no success. Then he turned to Caleb and asked, "Did she tell you why she's running?"

"I think she told me what she told you. She was wrongfully convicted. Her husband died owing drug dealers a bunch of money. That she has a young daughter who needs her. And she has a grandmother who is waiting for her to come. And then she said this strange thing about cutting her hair."

"I don't understand the hair thing," said Lou.

"Me either," Caleb said

Nate was finished packing. He looked at Caleb and gave the instructions, "You and Lou take the sheriff's truck back to his cabin and wait for me to call. I'm going to hope the steep mountains and the snow slow her down and that I can catch up with her and talk her into coming with us. I might be a few hours. I might be a few days, but I'll check in with you when I get cell phone service. Okay?"

"Okay," said Caleb. "What do I tell Marie?"

"I'll take care of Marie," Nate said.

Nate then pointed to the energy bar wrapper that had been left by the runner at the side of the truck. When Boo put his nose on it, Nate gave the "track" command. Boo then went nose down and followed the exact path the runner had followed. Along the road. Down the sagebrush slope. Across the grassy meadow and river then into the trees on the other side.

As soon as he disappeared, Lou shook his head in frustration and said, "That man has a head of cement and a heart of gold." Then he motioned for Caleb to get into the truck, and they drove back down the bumpy dirt road towards the main highway. As he did, they looked up in the trees along a side road and saw the nose of a black Jeep Rubicon poking out from the trees.

"I thought those guys would have given up by now," Lou said.

"I guess they think she knows something that she doesn't," said Caleb.

·　　　·　　　·

Two miles away, on the ridge above the meadow, Kwayah was making good time. She had followed a small, dry streambed up on a gentle rise to the ridge. She knew the ridge would lead her southeast towards Kermsuh Lake, though a light dusting of snow above ten thousand feet might slow her down. At Kermsuh Lake, she would shelter for the night. Then she would follow the trail down to the central fork and up to Ryder Lake, which was above timberline, and go over the pass into

Naturalist Basin. That would be her most strenuous day, she assumed, because it would include a dramatic climb and descent over a steep ridge. From Naturalist Basin, she would follow the trail to Rock Sea Pass then down the Duchesne River to Moon Lake. If she was lucky, she would catch a ride at Moon Lake to Fort Duchesne and arrive in time for the haircutting ceremony. It was the kind of cross-country backpacking route that would take fit and ambitious hikers five or six days to complete. But she believed she could do it in three nights and four days. She did not expect to be followed, not by Nate and his team, and not by Randy and Gare and the night guard crew who were trying to protect their enterprise. No one would follow her as she flew on foot through the summer hunting grounds of her people.

As she ran, she thought about Caleb. He was a good kid with a strong bond to the dog. When she was first in prison, feeling the deepest despair, she remembered reading his story and seeing him on the morning television news. He had a brave heart, and she hoped she would meet him again someday when she was not running.

A mile along the ridgeline, with Hayden's Peak to the south, she passed into the shadow of the hill, and the light snow dusting started sticking to the rocks. She knew she needed to slow down because the temperatures were dropping and the slushy week-old snow was freezing hard and becoming icy. A slip and an injury at this altitude, in this remote area, could be fatal. She slowed to a brisk walk until she reached the rock slides called scree fields, which she crossed slowly and with the utmost care. Her trail running shoes were named after famous Utah Mountains, and they offered good traction in these severe conditions, but she still needed to plan each step on the difficult terrain.

It took three hours to reach the Kermsuh Basin, less time than she expected. In the summer, it was a popular fishing and camping lake in the designated wilderness. But this late in the year, after the first high country snow, she expected no backpackers, anglers, or day hikers. A quick look at the trail in the fading sunlight proved she was right. With just a short bit of daylight left, she stayed on the trail and made another mile or two progress towards Ryder Lake. Running on the trail was like driving on a freeway after being on a dirt road. In the next mile, the trail dropped about a thousand feet back into the drainage of the Stillwater Fork. With her steady running rhythm, she pounded her way closer to her ohma at Fort Duchesne.

In thirty minutes, the light was gone, and Kwayah stepped off the trail with her miniature flash light and into a thicket of young spruce trees. She pulled together an enormous pile of boughs between two large fallen trees. She built a small fire then dug a trench next to the fire with a stick. While the fire burned to coals, she ate the last of her energy bars and drained a liter of water with a sports drink mix. Then she carefully raked all the coals from the fire into the trench and covered it with dirt, stamping down the loose soil with her feet. Finally, she spread the boughs carefully over the heated ground and climbed into her mylar sleeping bag fully clothed. She pulled her stocking cap over her head and felt the warmth from the broken earth below her transfer heat into her tired bones.

•  •  •

The runner had been soundly sleeping for an hour when Nate stumbled into Kermsuh Lake, feeling like he had aged thirty years in three hours. His boots were soaked and his left pant leg torn from a fall. His headlight batteries were dimming, but he was too tired to change them, so he pitched his tent in the first flat spot he could find in the warmer air away from the lake, rolled out his pad, and crawled into his sleeping bag. He didn't know if the runner was somewhere near the lake or miles ahead, and he was too tired to care. He was even too tired to cook a quick meal on his stove, so he ate a couple granola bars from his chest pack and settled in for the night. Boo found a patch of ground to warm up in the tent's vestibule, sleeping with his head buried in his tail. Some nights, Nate would hear him dreaming with muffled barks and other noises that he never made when he was awake. But not this night.

After a restless five-hour sleep, Nate awoke in the morning's gray. The air was still, and the clouds were thick and low, signaling to him the approach of a storm. His GPS signaled the same news, so he crawled out of bed, rolled up his kit, and shouldered his pack. Within a few minutes, Boo had picked up the runner's track again. It was leading straight down the trail and back into the Bear River Drainage. Was she circling back? Chickening out after a chilly night on the mountain, or was she going to turn southeast at the river and head towards Ryder Lake? Ryder was one of the highest elevation lakes in Utah. It sat behind Hayden Peak and over the ridge from Naturalist Basin. It was the most direct route to Fort Duchesne. When he came to the bridge in two miles, he would know if he was going up or down, if he would sleep warm or cold that night.

Near the bridge, where the stream from Kermsuh merged with the Stillwater Fork, Boo took Nate into a dense clump of new spruce trees. The dog showed him where she had built a makeshift shelter and bed and slept over a trench fire. Probably slept warm. He could see her foot prints in the small patch of snow in the shade. They were fresh, maybe an hour old.

With renewed energy, the deputy and his dog committed to the track. But to their disappointment, the track turned towards Ryder Lake and the daunting ridge on the far side of the bridge. They would spend another night, maybe two, on the mountain. To add to the concern, Nate could see all around him the signs of the first big winter storm. It was in the warmer than expected air and the lack of birds. In the large game wildlife, deer, and moose that had already moved to lower elevations. At this elevation, they were closer to the fast-moving clouds, and he wondered if the runner was seeing this too. He wondered why she was still running with confidence towards her home and her people.

It took until midday for Nate to get to Ryder Lake. When he did, he looked at the daunting ridge he would have to climb, taking him over eleven thousand feet to Naturalist Basin. As he crossed the outlet to the lake and studied which route would be best to ascend the ridge, Boo stood rigid. Sometimes his dog was like a pointer, and Nate followed the nose across the remaining stretch of the high valley and up the cliffs and boulder fields to see a lone woman in black slowly making her way up the last 100 feet to the top. It took a full five minutes for her to go the last hard steps over the ridge. Nate watched through his binoculars. She focused on each step, on what was in front of her, and when she reached the ridgeline, she went over without looking back.

Nate and Boo followed, keeping to her route up the steep slope. For the next three hours, they struggled up, over, and around boulder and cliff faces. At times, he had to lift the dog in his harness up to the next ledge or over a boulder, and at others, he had to take off his pack and tie his fifty-foot length of cord around it then hoist it up after he had successfully climbed up. It was nerve-racking and difficult, but finally, he reached the summit only to see a greater challenge ahead.

# CHAPTER 21

The storm clouds were charging at him like an angry witch from the southwest. From where Nate stood on the high point of the ridge, he could see the thick wall of clouds moving towards him from fifty miles away. The weather front had been pushing warm air towards him, but that was about to change. As the sun set, the temperature would drop thirty degrees over an hour, and another fifteen before midnight. The temperatures, accompanied by the wind, would show no mercy to any living thing exposed to their wrath.

With the weather before him, the accumulative exhaustion of the last thirty-six hours was like rocks in his pack, slowing him down and making each step difficult. He had to get off the ridge and down to the shelter of the trees below the timberline. As soon as he saw the storm, he stopped and dug into his pack. It was better to put on all his layers, his wool hat, and thick gloves now before the winter witch tried to knock him off his feet and steal his body heat. He quickly called Boo off the track, and the dog gave it up reluctantly. It was not time to worry about the runner but instead move with dispatch down the steep rock slide, around the cliff bands, and into the shelter of the trees. The runner's track would soon be covered with snow anyway.

As Nate moved slowly down the unforgiving slope, he worried about Kwayah. Nate's man-tracking skills told the story of her travels. He had seen her footprints in the snowfield on the upslope, and he believed she was an hour or two ahead. He could also tell by her stride she had slowed down. Her gait showed she was injured and favoring her left leg, as Lou had said. Still, she was moving and ahead of him. He hoped she would stop once she entered the trees and that Boo could find her by air scenting. The runner had much less gear than the overprepared deputy. He was dressed for winter travel, while she had lightweight but waterproof protection in the form of nylon layers. He had a light one-person tent and a sleeping bag good to ten degrees. She had a mylar emergency sleeping bag that just kept off the wind. He had an ultralight camping stove that could boil water in under two minutes. She needed a fire to cook or keep warm. Nate still had a package of jerky, some protein bars, three freeze-dried meal packets, hot chocolate, soup mixes, and hot dogs for Boo. He also had two large russet potatoes from Idaho wrapped in tinfoil. They were his favorite wilderness food. Simple to cook on a fire. Delicious to eat skin and all. In all, he had about four thousand calories of food. He assumed she had nothing left because he had seen places as he tracked where she had picked rose hips and scraped the inner bark of the aspen tree for the few calories they would yield. But before he could confront those concerns, he needed to make it to the tree line.

Nate's first attempt to descend the ridge ended in a near disaster. The sky was darkening, the wind was howling, and bits of frozen rain were lashing at his face when he came to the top of a cliff band. He only saw the hundred plus foot drop to the scree field below because Boo had stopped and was looking over the basin below, still tracking the runner with his nose. Nate had no time to scan the terrain and see what Boo was scenting. He would have to go around. Somehow, he found the strength out of necessity to scramble back up the mountain on his spent legs, move laterally across the slope, and descend at a safer point.

With just a few hundred feet of descent left, the storm hit with a fury. The wind assaulted his exposed face and sent a chill through his heavily perspiring frame. A few minutes more and he reached the base of the ridge, but he still had a half mile of gradually descending open country to reach the trees, which he could no longer see because of the blizzard. This was where his rarely used compass became useful. He took the compass from the chest pack of essentials he always carried. It was at the bottom of the pack and sticky from the energy bars and candy that always took priority at the top of the pack. Then he set a bearing due south. The chest pack had all the essentials so that even if he lost his full pack, he could survive. His chest pack had, he thought, about what the runner had. Matches, a knife, a small first aid kit, a map, the compass, some calories, a mylar blanket, a flashlight, and a few other things deemed "essential" for wilderness travel.

The compass told him which way to go, and he moved through the open country with ease. It had taken him several hours to go a mile over the ridge. Now he would cover the half mile between the base of the ridge and the forest in ten minutes. By the time he reached the trees, the wind speeds had dropped, and snow had become steady. He had about 100 feet visibility, so he couldn't see where it might be best to make a camp. He liked to camp near firewood, so he continued downslope another half mile until he found himself in a small clearing next to a large strand of dead trees. The trees would give him the steady supply of firewood he would need throughout the night.

The sun was completely gone now, and the moon and the stars were a thick cloud cover away. There was a boiling ocean of dark clouds overhead. Nate dropped his pack in a flat space next to a large boulder, paying careful attention to the location because it would be covered by the falling snow in a few minutes. He would build the fire next to the boulder and reflect the heat towards the tent. Because the snow was coming fast, he needed to collect firewood first, before it was covered with the first layer of big snow of the season. His tank was running on empty, but in the next twenty minutes, he gathered five large armfuls of wood and stacked then near the boulder. His rule was to always get twice as much wood as he thought he would need, except in the winter. Then get three times as much. Nate pulled a large trunk of deadfall into the fire pit. He would feed the thick wood into the fire during the night.

The snow and the wind would make a match-lit fire a slow process, and Nate didn't have the energy or the time to kneel, block the wind, keep the tinder dry, and nurture the flame. He roughly assembled small and medium-sized wood at the base of the boulder then took out one of two signal flares he carried in his search pack and pulled the top. The phosphorus flames burned bright and reflected across the new white covering. Nate held it up, and it cast an eerie red shadow reaching to the tops of the ghost like trees. Then he placed the flare in the starter fuel of the fire, and despite the falling snow and the wet, the wood quickly ignited. Before the flare had run its course, a full bonfire was raging. The wind captured the smoke from the fire and whipped it over the clearing and up into the trees.

The tent was next. Not too close to the fire because an errant coal could burn a hole in the side of his shelter. But not too far because the heat from the fire would reflect off the rock and give him a few extra degrees. He pitched his small ultralight tent on the flat space. It was not a winter tent, but it was certainly worth the two pounds of weight in his pack. In all, having a tent like that near the fire would help him sleep ten or fifteen degrees warmer and out of the wind.

Once the tent was up, he pulled out his lightweight sleeping pad and laid out his sleeping back. Nate used a bulky but lightweight plastic foam pad that could be used for other things as well. He had used it to make splints for injured hikers or even as material to fix a broken backpack. He often joked that with enough plastic foam pad and duct tape he could recreate almost any essential piece of camping gear.

Boo found the perfect distance between the tent and the boulder and claimed the space by curling up and placing his head under his tail. He was tired too, but he wasn't cold. Dogs almost always slept warm, even on the ice or in the wind. And golden retrievers were particularly good at weathering storms because of their furry coats. But to stay warm, they needed calories. Nate was prepared with a couple hot dogs and a dog biscuit. Later in the night, as the fire died, Boo would move closer to the warmth of the fire. He was always comfortable sleeping outside where he could protect the camp.

With fire and shelter ready, it was time for food. He boiled water with his stove and poured it into the freeze-dried meal. While the food absorbed the water, he made hot chocolate and soup. He needed all the strength he could get. Lastly, he carefully put his potatoes into the fire for a hot midnight snack. By the time he had downed dinner, the fire was providing needed warmth, and steam was pouring off his clothing.

The boulder, the tent, and the fire protected him from the wind and created a bubble of warmth. Before climbing into his small tent, he stood close to the fire and swapped out his wet clothes for some dry ones from his pack. By morning, those he'd taken off would be dry— and cold, but he'd live with that.

With his clothing dry and his stomach full, he unzipped the tent and climbed into his sleeping bag. He was surprised how the warm nest felt like home to him. He planned to rest for a few minutes then retrieve the potatoes and have a second feast. Instead, he fell instantly asleep.

In the early hours of the morning, after the storm had broken, Nate dreamed. In his dream he was at home, and he rolled over to touch Marie, but she wasn't there. Nate called Marie the woman of his dreams, but he rarely actually dreamed about her. In his dream, he couldn't touch her, but he heard her voice saying, "We have a visitor. There's a visitor at the door for you." The dream jumped forward, as dreams do, and he was at the front door of their simple well-kept house in Lincoln, greeting a friendly, faceless visitor, with Marie providing a welcoming embrace. He awoke with a start, sealed in his tent. The shadow of the fire, which should have been muted by now, danced across the nylon sidewalls. He could even feel the warmth as he realized the fire was burning at full strength. He unzipped the fly and stuck his head out to a surprising scene. The runner was sitting on a small rock as close to the blaze as was safely possible. Her body was drinking in the heat, but her face looked gaunt and weathered.

Nate was speechless. Whatever happened next, he didn't want her to continue to run. He sorted through his police scripts and the vocabulary of a good marriage and just couldn't find the words to break the stare down between the two. Finally, he pointed and said, "There are a couple baked potatoes with your name on them in the coals by that rock." Kwayah gratefully took a stick and rolled one of them out of the coals. She picked it up with her handkerchief and put it in her pocket. It would help keep her warm. Then she retrieved the second potato and tore off the tinfoil then split it open with a small knife so it would cool faster. As soon as it stopped steaming, she devoured it skin and all, ingesting the heat and the calories like a starving animal. Then she turned her attention to the second potato in her pocket. As she finished the second potato, Nate reached into his pack pocket and pulled out an energy bar. He tossed it to her, and she caught it with ease.

After a pause, he said, "Thanks for building up the fire."

"I was freezing to death," she said. "Couldn't get a fire going in the storm."

"How did you find me?" Nate asked.

"I saw the red glow of your signal flare. It was enough to get me going in your direction."

"So, you've been out in the storm for a while. You look like you are freezing."

"Better now. I dozed by your fire."

"More food?"

"I'm good."

Nate figured the longer he could keep her talking, the more likely she would stop running. But he remained in his tent with the nylon wall between them, afraid any movement in her direction would spook her like a wild horse. After a long silence, he said, "You need rest." She nodded affirmatively.

"It's a small one-person tent. Why don't you take a turn where I am, and I'll do a shift tending the fire?"

He could see in her face a longing for warm and soft and flat and sleep. But she wasn't yet brave enough to admit she didn't have any more run in her. Before she could answer, he stepped out of the tent and pulled his pants on over his shorts. He slid his sockless feet into his frozen boots and pulled his jacket on over his T-shirt.

As they exchanged places, he said, "We were in a bad way last night."

"Real bad," she said.

"We're okay now."

"Yes," she said. "We're okay now."

# CHAPTER 22

Nate slept some by the fire with Boo under his legs also radiating heat into his legs. Dogs average core temperature was well above humans, and it was one more way Boo subtly served his master. Still, Nate woke often, wondering about what would come next. He decided he would wait and gauge her reactions before he made a plan. Meanwhile, he hoped they had a shared priority to get out of the high-country wilderness as quickly as possible, before the next storm made any movement impossible.

While the runner slept in the tent until noon, Nate wondered what she would do when she awoke. He had not brought his handcuffs, so he could not constrain her. Besides, they were in a survival situation and needed each other. Also, he wanted the runner to know he trusted her to do what was right. For now, he'd let her sleep as much as she needed because they still had a long journey ahead of them that he hoped they would take together.

About six inches of snow covered the ground. The weather was overcast, which was good because a clear sky would mean colder temperatures. The best way out was to avoid the highway to the west, follow the snow-covered trail through the trees, and down to a junction with the famous Highline Trail. From there they would go up and over Rocky Sea Pass. After that, it would be a straight shot following the river downhill, twenty-six miles to the lodge at Moon Lake where he could get a cell signal and call Lou or Daisey Mae for a pickup.

After the sun came up, Nate gathered firewood and kept the fire going. While getting firewood, he found a five-foot-long straight shaft of spruce which he smoothed out with his pocket knife and created a walking stick for the runner. He hoped it would help take some of the pressure off her injured leg and ensure she didn't lose her balance in the slippery snow.

When Kwayah awoke, she stumbled out of the tent embarrassed she had slept so long. Nate greeted her with a mug of hot chocolate and a granola bar. She clutched the sleeping bag around her, even though she was fully dressed.

"Not much of a breakfast," he said in self-deprecation.

She looked at the sun then looked at Nate and said, "Lunch. It is lunchtime." Nate could see she knew the time of day, likely within fifteen minutes, by the position of the sun.

"If it's okay with you, we'll pack up and head towards Moon Lake." Nate just assumed they would hike together. He could see the runner was chilled, and he made a place for her near the fire where she could absorb the heat. Her slight frame and low body fat made her vulnerable to the cold.

"Your light windbreaker will not cut it," Nate said. "I've got an idea." Nate took the duct tape from his small emergency repair kit. Then he picked up the blue plastic foam sleeping pad and folded it end to end. Once he had determined the middle, he cut an oblong hole in the pad just large enough for her head to get through.

"Take off your windbreaker," he told the runner. She looked at him dubiously, but removed the light shell. Nate placed the sleeping pad over her head. Each end fell below her waist but above her knees. Then he took the duct tape and ran a strip around her waist, securing the pad around her core. For a final touch, he asked her to be still, and he slit small sections of the pad under her arms, allowing him to close the pad around her rib cage with tape. "Be careful with this. We might need the foam padding tonight if we're still out. Now, put on your windbreaker over your additional layer of insulation."

The runner did as she was told, but it took some effort to compress the padding enough to close the zipper on the windbreaker. When she finally did, she looked like she had gained fifty pounds. The windbreaker ended at her waist, but the flaps of the pad extended below her waist like a foam miniskirt. Kwayah smiled. The outfit provided instant warmth that had not been there moments before.

The runner had a lightweight stocking cap and a hood on her windbreaker. So, the next problem was gloves. Nate always carried extra socks. He took blue medical gloves from his first aid kit and put them on his hands. Then he took the extra wool socks he had slept in during the night and pulled them over as gloves. Then he handed her his warm winter gloves, and she accepted them with reluctance and appreciation.

"Once we get going, we'll warm up," the deputy said, something they both knew. Kwayah said nothing but looked at her feet. Throughout the morning, when the runner slept, Nate had carefully dried both sets of footwear and socks, heating them near the fire just enough so they would give up their moisture but not so much that they would be damaged by the heat. When she had crawled out of the tent, she was delighted to find her socks and running shoes dry and warm. But in the short time that they stood on the frozen ground, the cold penetrated the soles of the shoes, and her feet became cold again. Kwayah stepped close to the fire and moved her shoes as close to the fire as possible without being in the fire.

Kwayah reached inside the tent and pulled out the sleeping bag, carefully folding it up so it would not get snow on it. She suggested she carry the bag in her pack to more fairly share the load. Nate agreed. He pulled up the stakes and took out the poles, collapsing the tent. Then he stuffed it in its bag without much care. It was time to hurry. While he packed, Kwayah dropped her pack at Nate's feet and walked a few hundred feet out of sight into a clump of trees. After she had done her toilet without question, with privacy, Nate started to trust her more. Of course, there were still words that needed to be spoken, but that would come later.

Nate pulled up the GPS map on his cell phone and showed Kwayah where they were and how they would intercept the Highline Trail three miles to the south then follow the Highline to the Rocky Sea Pass. The pass would take them above timberline once again, but they would only be exposed for three miles. Then they would follow the Duchesne River down to the flat land, civilization, the reservation, and the awaiting danger.

For now, they were safe under the cover of first snow, following a trail that had been vacant for weeks. Nate led out in silence, but soon Boo assumed the lead. It was just the natural place for the dog at the front of the procession. Every once in a while, he would stop and let everyone pass him, touching the hand of each person with his nose as they did so. It was his way of checking in and making sure everyone was okay. Then he would assume his place at the front of the line again.

They headed south through the trees and over the deadfall, but after a mile, they came upon a trail of sorts that headed where they wanted to go.

The Rocky Sea Pass was more of a big lump than a ridged mountain. A free-flowing spring at the base had not frozen, and Nate and Kwayah filled up all their water bottles without filtering. The first few hundred feet up the pass were steep and slippery. The snow was getting deeper, but it was crystalized, light, and fluffy because it was so cold. After the steep section, the incline was gradual all the way to the top. When they finished their ascent, they could see a beautiful panorama framed by majestic peaks. At the same time, the sun peeked through the cloud and sent a flash of crystalline starbursts across the snowfields. It was so bright that Nate had difficulty looking and so beautiful that he could not. Both stood stunned by the beauty of the moment. Then the runner spoke.

"My grandmother taught me that beauty and fear are not opposites."

Nate understood. The snow, the cold, the exposure that could kill them if they didn't move was also beautiful beyond words.

"Your grandmother is wise," he said. "My father used to say heaven could not be more beautiful than the mountains in the West."

"He was wise too," she said.

After staring at the scene in silence for a moment, they walked on, but just before they disappeared into the trees, Nate heard the unmistakable sound of a small aircraft engine. He was surprised. He didn't expect to see a private pilot over the wilderness area at this time of year. Most prudent flyers would go around because they had to climb too high to clear the peaks and because no emergency landing options were available. But the engine persisted and came up over the Rocky Sea Pass flying low and slow. Nate recognized the type of plane. It was a Carbon Cub. A very lightweight plane made for mountain flying. Most were bought by Alaskan bush pilots, but in the lower forty-eight, a few were owned by millionaire hobbyists who liked the idea of being able to take off on a 200-foot runway. But most Carbon Cubs were owned by law enforcement agencies, used mostly for search and rescue.

Nate could see by the tail markings that this plane was law enforcement, but he said nothing to the runner. If the plane stayed in the area for long, he was pretty sure he could contact it with his multiple frequency radio deep in his pack. But Kwayah seemed nervous about the plane, so as it flew by going just sixty miles an hour, he waved and gave the pilot a thumbs up. The pilot clearly saw his gesture and wiggled the wings of the plane without changing directions. Within a few minutes, the plane was no longer in sight.

·     ·     ·

Inside the plane was Retired FBI Agent Lou Bertrum. After getting an earful from Marie Garner about Nate's plan to catch the runner, Lou had called his friend David Bennett from the Utah County Sheriff's Search and Rescue Team. Bennett was one of the best mountain pilots in the west and had a new Carbon Cub which he flew often. Bennett agreed to go on a "training mission" over the Uintahs. Along the way, he picked up Lou by landing on a straight stretch of Highway 150 near

Christmas Meadows, just a few miles from the Bertrum wilderness cabin. It took them just one pass to pick up the fresh tracks of a big dog, a deputy, and a runner going over the Rocky Sea Pass which they followed down the Moon Lake drainage.

After the fly over, Lou called Nate's wife, Marie. "He's all right. It looks like he has found her, and they're working together to get out. Still have a bit of a hike. We'll meet them tomorrow when they get to Moon Lake."

He also called Daisey Mae. "I'm not sure which local people we can trust on this, so let's share what we know with the Drug Enforcement Agency and the Bureau of Indian Affairs and see if we can get some help bringing them in."

·    ·    ·

On the ground, the party of two plus dog continued for another three miles until they came to an often-used elk camp. Because it was a designated wilderness, permanent structures were illegal. But the last elk hunters in the area, perhaps a month ago, had hauled in hay on pack animals for their horses. The hay had been left covered with a now tattered blue plastic tarp. They had also built a rock altar fireplace and left enough firewood for several nights.

Normally, Nate would have been angry with this kind of appropriation of the wilderness that was supposed to be pristine, but today he was grateful. He smiled and looked at Kwayah. She smiled too then pointed to cut marks made with a blade high up one tree.

"Those are the markings of my people who are telling other Utes this is a claimed hunting ground. We are on tribal lands." Nate knew the Ute Indian Reservation was on the south side of the Uintahs. But he learned only recently it was a checkerboard reservation with tribal lands scattered like islands in the ocean of the Uintah Basin.

The runner paused and looked down the trail they would travel the next day. Soon they would be below the snow line, and they would cross into tribal lands where she would feel safe. But tonight, they would eat all the remaining food. They would warm rocks by the fire and place them in the straw. Then they would sleep warm, her in the tent with the light emergency sleeping bag and Nate under the tarp with the warm sleeping bag. They didn't miss the plastic foam pad that had been carefully cut up as insulation for Kwayah that morning. Boo had already burrowed into the straw and was sleeping with his left front paw over his head.

In the twilight by the fire before they retired, the runner spoke to Nate the words long kept in her heart.

"My people grow fewer every year," she said. "We were once many, but disease and intermarriage took so many away. Our band are of the Northern Utes. Only 1,800 of us remain. Less than a hundred of us speak the words of our ancestors as I do. If I live long, I might be the last to speak the ancient words."

Nate watched the flames of the fire and listened with reverence. In the last twenty-four hours, he had watched patiently as they both learned to trust each other. He felt a bond with her, the bond only felt after surviving a near fatal experience with someone.

"You have asked why I am running. I am running from the wicked man who sells drug to children on the Wyoming reservation. I am running from the bad guards who let him sell drugs to prisoners. They will kill me if I am not silent. But they might also kill my daughter who is with my grandmother in White Rock. My Wici-ci is my only tie to my people, and she is in her last days. She has called me home, and I must go. When she dies, I must cut my hair and my daughter's hair and place the hair with her so she can pass into the next life connected to her family. This is our tradition."

Nate waited and watched as the fire slowly died. Then he said, "I don't know what will happen tomorrow. But I can promise you I will do everything in my power to make sure you have time with your daughter and with your grandmother."

Nate watched for a few more minutes then poured the last remaining hot chocolate envelope into their shared mug, filled the mug with hot water, stirred it, and handed it to her. As he did, he could see frozen tears on her weathered cheeks.

# CHAPTER 23

Eager to see their journey end, they both awoke as the sun was still over the horizon but the distant clouds were turning rose colored. There was no point in warming the fire because there was nothing left to cook. They hastily stuffed the tent and other gear into their packs, not bothering to put it in order for another night. His boots and her shoes were cold. They had not been carefully dried as they had been the night before. Kwayah chose to not wear the plastic foam vest that Nate had shaped the day before. It would not be as cold today, and they planned to move quickly. With packs loaded, they started walking. They had just eight, maybe ten, miles left to cover, and it was all downhill.

But the snow was heavy and melting as they arrived at lower altitudes, making the trail slippery and muddy. Both fell on their backsides during a steep descent where horses and hikers had worn the path. Nate was glad for the distraction of the hard conditions because he didn't want to ask what Kwayah planned to do when they reached the trailhead. He had promised he would help her visit her grandmother and daughter, and he wanted to protect her. But there were other forces at work. Rules and laws, and a trio of bad guys. Then there was the matter of the flyover. Was that a coincidence? Was it the good guys? Or was it an extension of the corrupt prison guards that were stalking the runner? Nate didn't know, but he didn't want Kwayah to worry about it.

By eleven a.m., they had covered almost eight miles, and they came to the north end of Moon Lake. The natural lake was dammed at the far end so it could store more water for downstream farmers. It was part of the massive Central Utah Water Project that directed flow from these remote parts of Utah to Salt Lake and Provo on the populated Wasatch Front. As a result, it had a clearly defined shoreline with a well-used trail on the west side and a lesser-used fisher's trail on the left side. From the north end of the lake, Nate couldn't spot any fishers or boaters on the lake. The trails skirted the half empty lake, weaving into the trees but leaving long, open patches around the edge of the lake. Nate assumed the lodge and cabins at the south end would be closed and all boarded up at this time of year. But he also assumed he might get cell service soon, so he took out his cell phone and turned it on. He was still out of range of service, but he kept the phone on, searching for a connection so he could check in with Lou as quickly as possible.

As they entered the open space at the north end of the lake, Boo's head abruptly came up. For a moment, he froze and would not let the two of them proceed. He was looking down the trail on the west side. Then he let out a deep growl reserved for warning of real danger. Nate stared down the trail and spotted a fresh boot print. On closer inspection with the binoculars, he could see it might have been made by the polished sole of a cowboy boot—the kind of boots worn by the man in black with the Jeep Rubicon. Without saying a thing, the two quietly retreated back up the trail to the cover of the trees.

After waiting a few minutes to see if anyone came their way, Kwayah said, "Let's go down the east side of the reservoir. That trail is not on the map. Boo is telling us there's an ambush on the west side." Nate agreed. He gave the dog the "haw" command, telling Boo to go first through the trees and brush. Nate knew Boo would warn them if he sensed another ambush on the east side. He hoped they could make it down that side and find help below the dam.

·　　·　　·

In the Lincoln County Sheriff's pickup truck, a half mile below the dam, Caleb was disappointed. Lou, who he liked in a big way, had parked concealed in a grove of cottonwood trees. As he and Daisey Mae prepared their weapons, Lou made Caleb promise out loud that he would stay out of sight of the dam and the truck.

"You need to promise you will stay over in those trees away from any action. I don't think bullets will fly, but you never know with bozos like these. I don't want you in danger. I also don't want you to see danger or feel danger. Good heavens, you're only twelve years old!"

"Thirteen," Caleb corrected the old man.

Daisey Mae sided with Lou. She looked mean in her bulletproof vest carrying an assault rifle, and Caleb used the moment to pass a jab back to Lou in a good-hearted way. "If I were a corrupt prison guard after someone ratting on me and my operation, I'd be more afraid of her," he pointed to Daisey Mae, "than of you. Especially cuz you're like eight-six years old."

"Sixty-eight," Lou corrected his new pal with a smile. "I'm a lean, mean sixty-eight."

Lou, Caleb, and Daisey Mae had driven three hours from Wyoming that morning. The day before, when Lou and his law enforcement friend Bennett had flown over the Rocky Sea Pass, they had seen Nate, Boo, and Kwayah making good time. Obviously, Nate was out of cell phone range. But several times since then, and after a call to another law enforcement friend, Lou had "pinged" Nate's phone. This had giving him a complete direction and rate of travel. So, they knew Nate and the runner were close to Moon Lake.

Local and tribal police officers and the Feds should have arrived by then to handle the operation. Lou and Daisey Mae were just "observers," though they were fully armed and outfitted for safety. Yet those officers were nowhere to be found. It was not like law enforcement to be late.

Then Lou received a surprise text from Nate. "Finally in cell range. Ambush set up on the west side of Moon Lake. Moving down east side of the lake out of sight. Where are you? Can you rescue us?"

He quickly texted back. "Daisey Mae and I will be on the east side of the dam at the picnic grounds. Expect reinforcements. Will let them deal with the bads. Acknowledge. Please."

"Copy," Nate texted.

With the truck parked out of sight, Lou and Daisey Mae headed stealthily towards the picnic grounds, but all Caleb could do was listen on the radio. The three were still using the family band walkie talkies because they were not authorized to use the operations frequency for the Duchesne County Sheriff, The Bureau of Indian Affairs Police, and the Federal Drug Enforcement Agency. Lou had tried to find the operational frequency that the feds would use on the mobile radio in Nate's truck, but he had no luck. The parade of agencies and officers was not because Kwayah was deemed dangerous, it was because those following her were. She had become a magnet for a group of prison guards and drug dealers hoping to cover up their bad business. She had become the bait.

The last thing Caleb heard Lou and Daisey Mae say before they left was, "We can't wait for the others to get here. They're in danger now."

Daisey Mae then said in the voice of an ex-Marine, "Let's go get them."

Caleb had promised to keep out of sight, but he had not promised not to watch. He was very good in the woods, very good at listening and knowing where people and animals might be. So, after stealthy moves through thick brush, he positioned himself a few hundred yards from the dam in full view of the picnic grounds. There he found a large spruce tree with ladder-like branches and climbed up twenty feet to have a perfect view. From this position he could see everything and warn Lou and Daisey Mae if he saw any problems. He also figured he could escape back to the truck without Lou and Daisey Mae ever knowing he had been there.

In position, he waited for what seemed like hours. Actually, it was about twenty minutes. Just past noon, things changed from slow to fast motion. First, Boo came busting out of the trees on the east side of the dam and immediately alerted on one restroom building. Nate and Kwayah followed but stopped when they saw the dog's warning behavior. They skirted around the structure towards the front of the dam, but they were dangerously out in the open. A short, stumpy woman dressed in camo and carrying a hunting rifle stepped out from behind the partition on the "Men's" side and called out to the pair. Caleb recognized her as the woman they called Gare—the night guard leader that Daisey Mae said was the ringleader and Kwayah said wanted her dead. Caleb couldn't hear what was said, but the pair stopped and held up their hands without turning around.

Boo didn't know what to do. He wasn't trained to be aggressive or to protect police officers, so he barked but stayed well away from the aggressor who was now standing twenty feet behind the pair.

Then Caleb clearly heard a different voice, a strong woman's voice. "Gare! You are pointing a loaded weapon at a deputy sheriff who is on duty. If you pull the trigger and survive my gunshot, you will die with a needle in your arm. Put the weapon down, or I will put you down." It was Daisey Mae. She stood at an angle so if she pulled the trigger on her assault rifle, Nate, Boo, and the runner would not be in the line of fire. Without turning around, Gare placed her hunting rifle on the ground. Daisey Mae quickly moved behind her and pulled Gare's handgun off her belt then shoved her to the ground. "I wish you had given me a reason to pull the trigger." The ex-Marine was mad. "Face down on the ground. Eat some dirt. Now!"

About that time, another of the prison guards came out of the trees on the west side of the dam. He was followed by another guard. Neither were armed and both were walking slowly and dragging their feet. From where he sat in the tree, Caleb was pretty sure one of them had wet his pants. Ten feet behind them was Lou. He was carrying two hunting rifles in one hand and his handgun in another. The pair were "politely" invited to lie on the ground next to Gare and share her meal. The three complained loudly using words that would get Caleb sent to his room for a week. He noted that Nate and Lou were equally gutter mouthed, communicating in language these lowlifes could understand.

But just when it looked like the whole thing was over, it got crazier. First, a helicopter flew over and made a quick landing on the dam. Three officers with weapons ready, dressed in black tactical gear and bulletproof vests, poured out the doors the instant the aircraft hit the ground. As they arrived, three large, black SUVs bounced into the picnic ground, stopped quickly, and officers exited with guns drawn. While that was happening, Caleb noticed five or six officers approaching on foot. One of them was just below his tree hiding place. Fortunately, the officer hadn't noticed Caleb. All the officers looked like what Caleb had seen on television. They were armed with ready assault rifles, handguns, and wearing helmets and radio ear pieces.

When they pulled in, Gare and her cronies didn't move. But Lou, Daisey Mae, Nate, and Kwayah did. Lou and Daisey Mae dropped their weapons out of reach and stepped back. Then all four of them placed their hands behind their heads and kneeled on the ground. Nate called Boo, who reluctantly came to a heeling position next to him. Caleb worried about what he was going to see next.

The leader, with a large, white letter on his vest, approached the four. He started with Daisey Mae. She stood up, opened her wallet, produced her identification, and was given the okay. She relaxed and took a dozen steps to the side. Nate was next, and he did the same. Then Lou. But the retired FBI agent and the man in charge embraced for a quick hug. Then it was Kwayah's turn. Daisey Mae intervened, asking the officer not to handcuff her. Then the two stood next to each other while the lead officer patted down Gare and the other prison guards.

About that time, Caleb heard Boo barking, not in the picnic grounds or on the dam but right below him. The dog who he loved had betrayed him with his affection. The entire group of officers on the assault team turned their attention on the dog and the tree, and Caleb was left with no option but to climb down sheepishly, walk through the picnic grounds, and face the smiles of his friends and surrounding officers.

"I thought I told you…" Lou scolded.

"I know. I know. I just wanted to make sure you all were all right."

Nate stepped over and gave the boy a fatherly hug. Then he said some reassuring words that went over his head because he was watching the next scene.

"Sorry for being late and for the body armor, big raid stuff," the man identified as the lieutenant said. "Probably a bit over the top. We got diverted when we passed this guy in the Jeep about three miles down the road. He's wanted by the DEA guys here." He motioned to some men standing around with DEA vests on. "And he had a whole pile of weapons and a supermarket of meth and other drugs stashed in a secret compartment in his Jeep. The tribal police," he motioned to the group of officers with the BIA vests, "are going to want him for intent to distribute.

"And if he's not having a bad enough day, he's also a suspect in a murder from his drug business on the reservation in Wyoming. Apparently, the Las Vegas police have evidence linking him to a murder for hire scheme involving a staged overdose three years ago."

The lieutenant then turned to Kwayah. "Are you the one who created all this fuss?" he said with a half-smile.

She said nothing.

"You are a brave woman," he said. "A generation of young people will be safer because of you."

Again, she said nothing.

"Cuch!" He called a BIA officer over. He was a young, well-groomed Native American man who clearly took fitness seriously. He was also a high school friend of Kwayah. One of many cousins from White Rock. Caleb could not hear the rehearsed words he spoke to her softly, but it was clear on her face what he said. Her grandmother was dead. Her tears came slowly, and Daisey Mae was the first to present her with a shoulder to cry on that turned into a full embrace of sympathy. Then Nate stepped forward. In his awkward way, he wanted to offer kind words at a difficult time, but Boo, sensing the emotion of the situation, nosed his way between them. Cuch interrupted.

"If we hurry, we can make it." He looked up to the dam, and the helicopter pilot gave him a thumbs up. Then the tribal police deputy handed Kwayah a carefully packed bag which she opened. "It's from Wici-ci," Cuch said.

"Oh, thank you," she said. Caleb watched as she trotted to the nearest camp restroom and quickly went inside. When she emerged just minutes later, she had transformed like a caterpillar to a moth. Her face was clean and fresh. Her hair was combed and tied with a beautiful yellow and blue ribbon. She wore a white full shirt that traveled below her waist and a multicolored ribbon skirt with three layers of yellow and blue ribbons that matched her hair ribbon. She quietly explained the dress had been a co-creation she had made with her grandmother for her high school graduation. On her feet were handmade leather moccasins with beadwork covering her toes that matched the beadwork medallion around her neck. Caleb could not help but think of how beautiful she was. As she turned and trotted up the hill to the dam, Caleb heard the helicopter engines warming up. Daisey Mae was already in position on the dam. She had taken off her tactical gear to reveal her dress uniform shirt. The two climbed into the back of the helicopter. Then Cuch said, "The rest of you, follow me."

As the helicopter launched and headed east, Boo bounded through the brush to the southwest and found the truck where he quickly claimed his favorite position in the back seat just behind Nate. Lou sat in the passenger's seat, and Caleb sat in back with Boo. They backed out on the road and pulled in behind a late model, black Bureau of Indian Affairs SUV with silver markings and a full light and antenna rack. Cuch flipped on his wig wag lights, and Nate did the same, following behind and driving fast but not dangerously. Solemnly, they headed over the county roads and past ranches towards White Rock.

"Have you ever been to a funeral before?" Nate asked Caleb.

# CHAPTER 24

The side doors of the chapel were wide open, and a gentle and needed cross-breeze brought the temperature down to a semi-comfortable level to the crowded pews. Sundays the chapel was half empty, half full, depending on who you asked. But today, the chapel was overflowing, and a PA system carried the sound to several large classrooms. The unusual heat on a late October day was compounded because it was 2:30 p.m., a full thirty minutes past the planned start time for the funeral. No explanation was offered.

Indians were often chided for taking a casual approach to the clock. But there was no "Indian time" at funerals. Utes took church seriously. The White Rock Chapel sat just three miles south of the High Uintahs on the edge of the high prairie. It was one of several religious denominations that had once been "missions" on the Ute Indian Reservation. Most Utes were members of a Christian church but also honored the old ways.

Grandma Wici had been a member of the White Rock congregation for eighty-seven years. Her name meant "song bird" in Ute, and her voice had graced the choir ever since her second naming when she was eight years old. As a child, she helped sew the curtains that were still used in the rectory and foyer. When she was a young adult, after a kitchen fire, she collected donations for new pots and pans from parish members. Those vessels would be used for the meal today. Every year, as long as she could remember, she worked with fellow church members to put together Christmas care packages for the poor in the community. And there were many poor people in the community.

Every person who had ever received a Christmas package, a kind word, a favor, or a piece of priceless wisdom from Grandma Wici attended her funeral. The small parking lot was full, with trucks and a few cars lining the main road in the small town. Civic leaders from Roosevelt and Vernal and tribal leaders from Fort Duchesne had also come. The funeral would last an hour then horse riders would pull a wagon with the casket a few miles north into the mountains to the place where the White Rock River spilled out into a mountain meadow. It was a sacred place of transition where another ceremony would take place, attended by close family members and friends. Then those who were close to Grandma Wici would cut their hair, a symbol of the time spent with the honored dead, a way to remember the wisdom of her words.

In the White Rock Chapel, the congregation assembled on time, singing all verses of "How Great Thou Art." But the preacher leading the service asked the congregation to sing another hymn then another. Something was going on, but nothing was said.

After thirty minutes of stalling, the congregation heard the loud unmistakable sound of a helicopter flying over the chapel. The engine sound shifted as the aircraft approached for a landing in the parking lot of another church. The congregation heard the engine shut down on the helicopter, and a few minutes later, Kwayah appeared at the back door of the small chapel in the ribbon dress she had made with her grandmother. She looked over the congregation and looked at the front of the chapel where her family was seated facing the casket. As she walked towards the front row where a place had been saved for her, a three-year-old girl stood up on the pew. She had the same blue and yellow ribbon in her hair and a miniature version of the ribbon dress that Kwayah wore. She looked at the approaching woman then pointed and said, "Pai-ni, pai-ni!" Kwayah broke into a run, stretching out her arms and embracing her child.

The congregation was directed to sing "Nearer My God to Thee," but most of the community who had witnessed the reunion had a lump in their throats or tears in their eyes, and it was not until the second verse did they recover enough to stay on key. As the congregation muddled through the classic Christian hymn, a tall, tough-looking woman in a rumpled Wyoming Prison Guard dress uniform stepped into the chapel. There was no place to sit, so she joined others standing against the back wall.

Halfway through the service, another group entered and stood in the back of the small chapel next to the warden. A Wyoming deputy sheriff dressed and smelling like he had just come out of the mountains from a three-day hunting trip, a tall well-kept older man who looked and walked like a "fed," and a young teenager who looked uncomfortable and curious at the same time. The overflow at the back of the chapel adjusted to let them each find a piece of wall to lean on.

•    •    •

Caleb had expected the funeral to be sad, with open tears and crying. But it was not. The speakers, which included a younger brother, a granddaughter, and a friend, talked about the joy this elderly woman brought to their lives. The preacher was the final speaker.

"Grandma Wici always carried the Creator in her heart as she cared for us. By 'us,' I mean everyone in this room. She believed we are all children of the Creator, and she took seriously the charge to care for His children, so she cared for us." He told inspiring stories of people and families Grandma Wici had served. Then he referred to the Bible. "The Apostle Paul was the author of her favorite scripture," he said. "In the Second Book of Timothy, first chapter, verses six and seven we read, 'Wherefore I put thee in remembrance of the gift of God that is in thee by the laying on of my hands. For God has not given us the spirit of fear, but of power and of love and of a sound mind.'

"I cannot say that Grandma Wici was never afraid. But when she was, or when I was, she would remind me of that scripture. She told me once, quite casually, that when she died, she hoped to meet Paul and thank him for his wise words."

At the conclusion of the preacher's words, which was not the sermon Caleb had expected, the preacher invited anyone who wanted to speak to say a final "goodbye." No one moved at first, but then one family member and another stood, walked to the pulpit, pulled the microphone to their face, and said kind things. A few short stories were shared about kind acts that arrived at just the right time and changed a life for good. And stories of wisdom spoken at the right time in the right way so that a life decision could be made.

But the only thing that would be remembered was what the last speaker said. She was a three-year-old girl with a blue and yellow hair ribbons who was holding her mother with both arms. The mother turned sideways so the child could speak into the microphone. Without fear, the little girl looked at the flower-covered coffin, and speaking directly to what was in front of her, she said quietly, "Thank you, Grandma, for being my mommy until my mommy could come home."

After a final hymn and a final prayer, the front doors of the chapel were opened to a glorious fall afternoon. There was a short pause as the people in traditional Ute dress exited the chapel. As the pallbearers from the family carried the casket out the side door, Caleb heard the soft rhythm of a drum and the chants of a Ute song. It was unlike the church hymn that had just been sung. There was no pipe organ, no familiar melody. But it had the same spirit. He could not understand the words, but he imagined they were words of power, of love, and of a sound mind. The family exited behind the pallbearers, and as they did, they joined in the chorus. The voices rose as the singers lined the sidewalk and opened a line for the procession to place the casket on a waiting horse-drawn wagon. Several young men and a young woman sat on horses in traditional wear, ready, and the invited guests began walking towards the mountains while singing. At the front of the procession was a young woman and her three-year-old daughter.

As Caleb stood between Nate and Daisey Mae, watching the procession, a young native woman in a ribbon dress approached the warden. "Are you Daisey Mae?" she asked.

"Yes," said the warden, surprised at being recognized.

"Kwayah wanted me to ask you if you would join her and her family at this time."

Daisey Mae swallowed her surprise and looked at her wrinkled garb. Realizing how significant such an invitation was, she looked at the young woman and said, "Yes, I would be honored."

Then the young woman nodded at Nate, Lou, and Caleb. "Please join us," she said.

The procession wound through the town to the sagebrush flats then along the river and into a tribal campground marked with "No Trespassing" signs. It was an easy three-mile walk for many, but Nate was still exhausted from his long trek across the mountains, so he found a place in the bed of one of the few pickup trucks following behind for stragglers. A horse rider had pulled Kwayah's little girl up in the saddle and made her feel like she was riding the horse by herself. Her mother walked next to the saddle, towards the mountains, holding the little girl's hand.

·   ·   ·

In the campground by the meadow, fingers of the river split apart then came together again. Kwayah remembered the time she had stood in that exact spot with her Grandma Wici and asked why her parents were not there for her. Her grandmother wisely said," Look at the river. See how the waters enter the meadow together, then split apart, then rejoins the other channels. But when the river leaves the meadow, it is a river again. That is the way of families."

In the second ceremony at the fire circle, the mourners took part in the sacred hair cutting, each taking a length of hair that represented the time they had spent with Grandma Wici. Kwayah cut her waist length hair all the way to her shoulders, then did the same with her daughters hair. The beautiful black strands dropped onto the dusty ground and mixed with the salty tears. Then the riders took the wagon down the mountain and the family lingered. Kwayah met many cousins, relatives, and friends as they ate buffalo burgers and sang songs. When the last pink light sank below the horizon and the flames of the fire were the only light, little girl's head became heavy, her eyes drooped, and she fell asleep with her mother's thigh as a pillow. Daisey Mae sat next to her on the log bench, quietly digesting the beauty of the day.

"I wish I had known your grandmother," she said in a soft voice.

"I wish she had known you," said the runner.

Then Daisey Mae seemed to unburden a weight she had been carrying for a long time. "I should have taken you out before things got bad," she said. "Before Gare put you in her sights. Before it was so dangerous."

There was a long pause then Kwayah said, "Both of us knew something was wrong, but neither of us knew who to trust."

"That is true. I didn't know where I could send you to be safe, so I kept you as close to me as possible. It was a poor decision."

Kwayah took her friend's hand with her right hand and ran her left hand through her daughter's hair. "We are all safe now," she said. "We are all safe now."

# CHAPTER 25

"Good morning. Okay. I'm sorry. Good afternoon. My name is Judge Will Ritter. I reside in Denver in the Federal District Court with authority over Utah and Wyoming. That's where all the participants in this hearing reside and are joining us via Zoom. I'm going to let you introduce yourselves in just a minute. But first, I need to describe for the record what we are doing here today." Caleb looked at the video screen carefully and could see that the judge had his exercise clothing underneath his black robe. His Nike running shoes were carefully hidden under his desk. He was giving up his lunch break and exercise period for this hastily organized gathering.

"This is an informal hearing. Did I say 'informal'? Nothing I say or do for the next thirty minutes will be legally binding. But I hope we will reach an agreement, and I hope we will all be big boys and girls and live up to the agreement so we don't have to waste the court's time with formal hearings, court orders, and other costly activities. Even so, we are recording this session and transcribing it so we can refer to our informal agreement in the future if needed. Thank you, Martha."

The judge nodded at someone off camera. Everyone on camera in an official capacity in the hearing gave an exaggerated nod into the camera so the judge could see.

"So, the objective of this meeting is to come to an agreement with the diverse parties in the video conference on how we will proceed to facilitate justice in a way that does not cause further harm."

There were more nods, though a prosecutor from Fremont County appeared skeptical.

"Finally, before introductions, I want to thank my good friend Lou Bertrum for calling this court's attention to this matter and suggesting a way we could help."

The judge nodded at Lou who was one of the postage stamp size heads in the row of Zoom participants.

"Twenty years ago, when we were both a little younger, Lou and his team quite literally took a bullet for me when the wife of a defendant in my court decided I was responsible for her husband's bad behavior. Thank goodness for poor marksmanship and good body armor. No one was hurt in that incident. The lovely woman who pulled the trigger was lucky enough to score a life sentence in the same facility where her husband is serving time. Occasionally, they get to see each other through the chain-link fence, which is nice. Unfortunately, someone else is raising their children. But I will always appreciate Lou for stepping in front of me at just the right time."

The judge raised the water flask he had prepared for his exercise session to his lips like he was making a toast, and Caleb, who was watching the procedure with Nate from a conference room in the Duchesne County Sheriff's Office, saw Lou Bertrum smile. Now it had been officially acknowledged that he pulled the strings to fast track a solution to this problem and help Kwayah.

"Now," said Judge Ritter, "let's get on to introductions because I'm expected back in court in thirty minutes on a matter that most of you are following in the media. Let's start with our friends in Utah and go from federal to state officials. Then Wyoming. Then we'll introduce counsel and the defendant."

The order of introductions had been listed in the chat box of Zoom, and the federal agents from Utah jumped in.

"I am Corporal Carson Cuch of the Bureau of Indian Affairs, currently stationed in Ft. Duchesne, Utah."

"I am Agent 237 of the Drug Enforcement Agency, also in Fort Duchesne, Utah." It was audio only. His camera was turned off.

The judge jumped in, "Agent 237, we can assure you that your identity will not be made public. We know how dangerous your job can be, and we all thank you for your service." Then he continued "Now I understand that neither of your agencies are charging the defendant. Right?"

Cuch nodded. But Agent 237 added, "The defendant has provided important evidence in an ongoing investigation into drug distribution in the Wyoming State Women's Minimum Security Penitentiary and also on the Shoshone Reservation. She has agreed on her own volition, your honor, to testify in these cases if needed. Our only concern is that she be placed where she cannot be harmed or intimidated as these investigations move forward."

"Noted," said the judge. Then the introductions continued.

"I am Sheriff Scott Mitchell of Duchesne County, Utah."

"Mitchell," the judge said enthusiastically, "the trout still biting at Starvation Reservoir?"

"Yes, sir."

"I don't believe you. I'm going to have to come out there and check as soon as the ice freezes thick enough so that this federal judge can walk on water."

"We'll be waiting for you, your honor," said the sheriff. "I expect you'll need an escort from the highest level of law enforcement in this county," he said with a smirk.

The judge laughed then continued, "And the defendant has committed no crime in your jurisdiction?"

"No, sir."

"Okay, Wyoming."

"I'm Sheriff Rondo Mathews of Uintah County, Wyoming." The judge nodded.

"Sheriff, you initiated the search for the defendant when you were notified that she escaped, right?"

"Yes, your honor."

"Does your agency or any agency in the county you represent plan to charge the defendant with any crime at this time?"

"No, your honor." Then he said in a good-natured way, "We might give her a medal."

The judge didn't smile, signaling he was the only one allowed to inject humor into the proceedings.

"Next, please."

"I'm Warden Daisey Mae Cromwell, Wyoming State Corrections." Daisey Mae knew how to speak directly to a judge and give as much information as possible with as few words as possible. Nate followed the example.

"I'm Nate Garner, Deputy Sheriff in Lincoln County, Wyoming."

"You're the tracker with the dog?" the judge asked.

"Yes, sir."

"And that's your junior deputy who is a guest in these proceedings sitting behind you?" Caleb had been told to be invisible, so he squirmed and was suddenly very uncomfortable. The judge said, "Please thank him for his service and remind him that what happens in a hearing like this stays in a hearing like this."

Nate and Caleb nodded. Then the final introduction.

"I am Dwayne Tanner, County Prosecutor for Fremont County, Wyoming."

"Thank you all," said the judge. "You already know Lou Bertrum who has absolutely no official standing in these proceedings. But I'm letting him watch anyway. Besides, he's retired and spends his time fishing. And you all know the defendant in this hearing because we have no other title in legalese to describe her. I have asked, no, ordered my former partner Jacob Vanderclout to represent her because she needs an aggressive counsel who will help to unravel this legal spider web over the next few months. But in the next few minutes, we need an agreement so this bad situation won't be worse."

The judge paused but not long enough that anyone could insert themselves into the proceedings that were gathering steam like a parting train.

"It is my understanding that the defendant was helping the warden with an investigation. Ms. Daisey Mae, could you please give us the short version of this, keeping in mind we are all pressed for time."

Daisey Mae rose then, noticing her head was no longer framed in the Zoom shot, sat down and scooted towards the camera.

"I first met Kwayah in Rawlings in her prison orientation. She was an unusual inmate. She listened and did exactly what we asked. Because of that, I asked to have her transferred into Evanston when I was named warden. There she took advantage of our educational programs and running in the exercise room every day. As we talked about her life plan, she didn't complain or deny, and because of that, she seemed like she didn't belong in prison. Once she could trust me, she began sharing information about how drugs were being smuggled into the prison. She was concerned that some of her fellow inmates who had fought hard to get clean were getting hooked again on meth and other drugs before they were released back into society. She provided very valuable information, but I needed more to make a case and have the charges stick. When she gave me more, she also asked me to look into her case. So, I began to check around. Unfortunately, the people in Fremont County were not very forthcoming."

"Objection, your honor!" Prosecutor Dwayne Tanner broke in.

"Cool your jets, Mr. Prosecutor," the judge said. "You'll get your turn. Meanwhile, I want to remind you that you are in an informal proceeding being mediated by a federal judge. A federal judge who takes a very dim view of prosecutors and lower court judges who try to cover their mistakes." The prosecutor huffed and was silent.

"Continue, Ms. Cromwell."

Daisey Mae continued her well-rehearsed statement. "I was able to gather some evidence from other sources that suggested Kwayah was pressured into taking a plea deal by her own attorney, a public defender who was aligned with her deceased husband's drug supplier. Beyond that, very little evidence exists on the record that a crime was even committed. By the way, your honor, I will call her by her name because I do not believe she should be a defendant. Kwayah tells me she acted in self-defense and to protect her daughter. The record should also reflect that the victim she allegedly attacked in this case is in the custody of the DEA who will be charging him with multiple crimes related to weapons, narcotics distribution, and possible conspiracy to commit murder."

The judge was surprised, and he asked the unseen DEA agent, "Is that right?"

"Yes, your honor," the blank face spoke.

Then Daisey Mae continued, "This is where I made a terrible error that could have cost Kwayah her life. She passed a note to me that said she believed the night guards in the prison were on to her. On to us. When I asked her for a few more weeks to gather evidence, I broke her trust. She broke out in order to save herself."

"Thank you, Warden," said the judge.

"We have heard from a trusted public servant about a difficult situation in one of our prisons. I also understand you are a combat veteran? A former Marine?"

Daisey Mae nodded.

"Thank you for your service, ma'am."

The judge continued, "Based on the evidence before this group, and because we are all interested in justice, I would like to suggest that Mr. Tanner and his office take a careful look at this conviction. Because this is not a formal hearing, and because I am serving in the role of a mediator, I cannot compel Mr. Tanner's office to do so. But I can ask, and ask nicely, is your office interested in reviewing this conviction, Mr. Tanner?"

"Your honor." Tanner looked at his notes. He was well prepared to make an argument. But the judge cut him off.

"Mr. Tanner, a 'yes' or 'no' will suffice."

Tanner looked like a slowly deflating balloon at a birthday party.

"Yes, your honor. We will re-investigate and reconsider."

Then the judge stepped further. "Please send my regards to the people in your office and ask them to provide me and Ms. Cromwell with a complete record of your findings within twenty-one business days. That should allow you and your staff enough time to get it right. Correct?"

"Yes, your honor," Tanner whined. The balloon was completely out of air.

"Also, please include Ms. Kwayah's counselor Mr. Vanderclout in that email chain. His firm will be contacting you and following your progress. Now, to the most important matter.

"It seems like the defendant will need to remain in someone's custody until this whole big mess gets cleaned up. And I'm told she has a particularly important responsibility." There was a pause and the little girl was displayed on the screen for the court to see. "Because she's a potential witness for the DEA, and because she deserves our appreciation, let me say admiration, for putting herself at risk to gather evidence, we need to have a very careful solution.

"In the interest of her protection, I would like to excuse Mr. Tanner. Communication with the defendant can be made through Mr. Vanderclout's Denver office. We will also excuse Lou. He needs to get back to fishing, or golf, or whatever you retired people do. Our DEA and BIA agents also have more pressing matters. I am sorry, but the fewer people who know where she is, the less likely we will have a leak. Sheriff Scott and Mathews, you can go back to your business, too."

The judge waited while the parties named dropped off the Zoom call. Then he started up again, "It's my understanding that Deputy Garner has proposed a solution that you have all agreed upon. Deputy?"

Nate cleared his throat. "Wyoming Corrections has agreed to release their prisoner to the Lincoln County Jail which is north of Uintah County in Wyoming. It's a very small jail, your honor. And we do not have a devoted area for women. So, when we have a woman prisoner, we either send her to a neighboring county, or if she's not a flight risk, we put her on work release."

There was a chuckle among the crowd as they could all see where this was going. Even Kwayah broke into a smile as she realized she would not be going back to prison. The question of her daughter was her next concern.

"There is a small dairy farm in our county that has a solid track record of helping women prisoners get back on their feet. We have arranged for Kwayah and the girl to have room and lodging on a ranch under the supervision of Kathy McConkie. Ms. McConkie is disabled and works from her power chair, but she and her husband can provide safe lodging out of view from the public until these legal matters are concluded and for as long as is needed afterwards."

"A safe haven," the judge said. "With good fishing nearby," he added. "I hope they have room for me when I retire."

"Are you good with this?" the judge addressed Daisey Mae.

"Yes, your honor."

"So, we have agreed that no one will bring any escape related charges, and we will hold the defendant on the McConkie Ranch until she can safely return and live in White Rock. That's a win-win," said Judge Ritter with a conclusive voice.

"Thank you, Judge," Kwayah said at the same time as others.

Then, like most judges, he wanted to be the last one to speak. "Ms. Kwayah," he said in a fatherly tone," I am sorry for the loss of your grandmother. I am also sorry you were served up some questionable justice that we are working to reverse. I am sorry we did not hear your story from your mouth today. It is a story worth telling. As a federal judge, I cannot give you legal advice. But your lawyer, Mr. Vanderclout, will advise you to tell your story to a judicial committee run by the Bar Association in the State of Wyoming. That would be the first step in a monetary settlement that will not begin to cover the pain and heartache you have suffered. But it will give you and your beautiful daughter a start."

There was a pause as the judge collected his emotions. "This hearing is adjourned."

# CHAPTER 26

It was early summer in Lincoln County, and the wild flowers were in bloom in every pasture and meadow. The streams were running full, emptying the mountains of snow pack. Caleb had just arrived for his annual six-week summer visit with Nate and Marie, expecting another summer of adventure with Nate and Boo and his friends. Eight months previous, in the Fall, he had flown into Salt Lake City and immediately been launched into an adventure searching for Kwayah, a Native American woman who was now his friend. To welcome him to his home away from home, Kathy McConkie had arranged one of her famous Sunday dinners to die for. Caleb was sure he could smell her famous pies cooking in the oven the moment he piled into the back seat of the pickup with Boo, even though they had a thirty-five-minute ride to the ranch.

When they arrived, Marie went directly to the kitchen to help and Caleb to a chair at the long dining room table. When he was joined by the others, Kathy rolled her power wheelchair into the dining room with the Elk meat roast on a tray on her lap. After the oohs and aahs of the guests, she pulled her power chair into the space by her husband. Just a few years before, Sunday dinner had been lonely affairs. The older couple were descending into isolation at their remote ranch in Lincoln County. Then last year delivered Marianna. She now lived happily in the bunkhouse and thrived helping with the hard work around the ranch. Eight months ago, they got a double bonus. A kind Ute mother and her child who also needed a low profile came to live in their revolving door family. The child, who they called Tuani, was now an active and articulate four-year-old. The yard in front of the ranch had been transformed into a playground where Kathy could keep her eye on the girl while her mother worked in the barn or trimmed the fruit trees.

On this day, it was Boo, the search and rescue dog, who had made this all happen, roaming the yard. He would get the elk steak leftovers later. His handler, Deputy Nate Garner and his wife, Marie, had contributed fresh sweet rolls still warm from the oven. Warden Daisey Mae had driven up from Evanston with news that the night guards had turned on Gare who had plead guilty and been sentenced to prison in Rawlins. Others had been placed on probation or fired. Lou Bertrum had arrived early in the morning and had contributed to the meal his fly-fishing trophy trout taken from the Lincoln River just an hour before. The nine-inch fish represented his first success fly fishing but provided only two bites to eat. Marianna came in shyly from the bunk house and joined the gathering who filled the dining room of the old ranch house.

Kathy said grace and choked back a tear as they held hands in a circle around the bountiful table and together gave thanks for food, freedom, and friends. It was a beautiful prayer. Caleb reached for one of Marie's fresh rolls, not disappointed that it was still warm. He had already sampled several on the ride from Lincoln to the ranch. The small talk and banter started, with much chiding of Lou and his little fish. There were polite questions for Caleb about his school year, the progress of his father's PhD, his mother's job, and whether or not he had a girlfriend at age fourteen. Kwayah and her daughter sat with Marianna at the far end of the table and drank it all in.

After a while, the conversation turned serious. Kwayah found a pause in the conversation to say in her quiet voice, "I'm going to start college at the University of Wyoming next year. I have a track scholarship and an opportunity to study my native language." There were broad smiles around the table, but then the questions turned practical. She said, "The money paid to me by the State of Wyoming for the time spent away from this little angel will be enough for us to get our own apartment and have some childcare."

Applause broke out around the table; then Kathy spoke. "Our Ute daughter and this little one will be welcome at the ranch any time. We will keep their bunk house apartment ready for their visits."

Marianna reached over and hugged Kwayah and then the little girl.

·   ·   ·

"Wici-ci."

The name tip-toed off her tongue into the autumn air then was stolen by the breeze.

The young woman, again. Softly. "Wici-ci."

The four-year-old child stood by the river with her mother and received her second naming. Fall leaves drifted in the ripples. In a quiet voice that penetrated the sound of rushing water, her mother placed the sacred name between them. Then she squeezed the girl's trembling hand.

"In your first naming, you are Tuani. It means "my child" because you live in the world but also in my heart. Now your second naming is what you are becoming."

The words came to the daughter's ears, into the young one's heart, and were engraved on her soul.

"Out of respect, we do not speak the names of the dead. I do not speak the name of my grandmother because she lives in a sacred place. But now you are Wici-ci. You are the songbird. As we speak your name, we will feel her spirit and your spirit grow in our hearts.

# ABOUT THE AUTHOR

When Author Scott Hammond and his search dog Boo are not looking for lost people, he's writing about them. If called, they will come with team members on the worst day of your life. If they can, they will find you, rescue you, and bring you home. Boo is a half English half American Golden Retriever who loves cheese and especially loves bringing closure to the families of the missing. Scott likes cheese too. An international expert on search and rescue teams, he recently solo hiked across central Iceland. He's a grandfather of eleven children. Every one of them is his favorite.

# SEARCH AND RESCUE DOG SERIES

# NOTE TO READERS

I spoke with many Ute friends seeking advice about how to make this book authentic and true to a culture and people I admire. Putting Ute language into English text is inherently difficult. First, Ute is an oral language not meant for the characters we use in a book like this. Spelling is problematic. For example, Evanston Wyoming is in Uintah County. The Uintas (without the "h") are the wilderness mountains on the northeast border of Utah and the traditional hunting grounds for the Utes. Fort Duchesne is in Uintah County, Utah. To avoid confusion for the casual reader, I made a fiction writer's choice and used one spelling (Uintah) for the Wyoming County and the Mountains. Then I moved Fort Duchesne in Uintah, Utah, to Duchesne County, Utah. Second, there are three bands of Ute Indians in Utah and Colorado. The White Rock/Fort Duchesne based band is one of the three. Each has a different dialect in a similar oral language. The Mountain Ute band in Colorado's dialect is more accessible to non-native speakers because it has a translation app. Finally, there are only a few native speakers left in any of the bands, and it is assumed that within a few generations, the language will be dead. Because of these problems, I hope the names that I chose and the descriptions that I made are as close to accurate as a non-native can be. I also hope the reader sees the quiet strength of this noble people.

# NOTE FROM SCOTT HAMMOND

Word-of-mouth is crucial for any author to succeed. If you enjoyed *Finding the North Wind*, please leave a review online—anywhere you are able. Even if it's just a sentence or two. It would make all the difference and would be very much appreciated.

Thanks!
Scott Hammond

We hope you enjoyed reading this title from:

www.blackrosewriting.com

Subscribe to our mailing list – *The Rosevine* – and receive **FREE** books, daily
deals, and stay current with news about upcoming
releases and our hottest authors.
Scan the QR code below to sign up.

Already a subscriber? Please accept a sincere thank you for being a fan of
Black Rose Writing authors.

View other Black Rose Writing titles at
www.blackrosewriting.com/books and use promo code
**PRINT** to receive a **20% discount** when purchasing.

www.ingramcontent.com/pod-product-compliance
Lightning Source LLC
Chambersburg PA
CBHW051230210726
48290CB00003B/879